Olusola Sophia Anyanwu is British Nigerian. She did all her schooling at Ibadan and studied Education in English at the University of Ife, Nigeria (now Obafemi Awolowo University, Ife). She served her National Youth Service Corps in Makurdi in Benue State, Nigeria, and taught English and Literature for 20 years in a federal school for girls in Port Harcourt. She relocated to the UK in 2003 and continued as an educationist in primary and secondary schools in the UK.

She is the author of *Stories for Younger Generations*, *The Confession*, *The Crown*, *Turning the Clock Hands Backwards* and *Their Journey*. She currently has other unpublished manuscripts in the making.

She is a devoted Christian, married to Emmanuel and blessed with many children and grandchildren. She lives in South East London with her family.

Dedicated to my precious grandchildren: Olanna, Ivana, Chima, Chioma, Gabrielle, Ariella and Caleb, and my future generations.

Olusola Sophia Anyanwu

STORIES FROM THE HEART

For Older Generations

AUSTIN MACAULEY PUBLISHERS™

LONDON • CAMBRIDGE • NEW YORK • SHARJAH

A CIP catalogue record for this title is available from the British Library.

ISBN 9781398419308 (Paperback)
ISBN 9781398419315 (ePub e-book)

www.austinmacauley.com

First Published (2021)
Austin Macauley Publishers Ltd
25 Canada Square
Canary Wharf
London
E14 5LQ

A big thank you to my most senior brother, pastor and elder Babatunde Adebayo for encouraging and prophesying success into my writing career. Also for his reading the book and giving a review: "It is well-written and shows the clear and deep mind of the author in telling captivating stories. The author is a consistent and powerful storyteller."

I am also thankful to the period of my undergraduate years at the University of Ife, Nigeria (September 1977 to July 1981) and my Youth Corps Service in Benue State, Nigeria (July 1981 to July 1982) when I wrote most of these stories to kill boredom.

I am deeply grateful to my loving husband, Emmanuel, for devoting time to give his useful suggestions and advice.

Table of Contents

All honour to God who shows me unfailing love.

Preface

This book is written for the purposes of reflection, humour and entertainment. Also, it is hoped that readers from every race, especially Nigerians, will derive some awe, nostalgia and even amazement at how life in the university, city, village and work life over 40 years ago differ so much from how these aspects of life are currently experienced.

Chapter 1
Teddy Boy

How priceless is your unfailing love… **Psalm 36:7**

His mother's name was Kizzy—a beautiful and smart thing, sweetly figured with a common but attractive blend of black, brown and white colours from head to feet. The father was Zambesi—a darkish brown, big, harmless brute, very sensible and calm. Teddy was born to them on the twelfth day of July. He had six brothers and ranked the fourth position. He was not the loveliest, but he had his own special qualities. He was a very big baby. With time, he even appeared to be bigger than his brothers. He lived in Ibadan, in one of those modern settings in Ibadan town. His family depended on and lived with a respectable couple who had their own children too.

Teddy's parents worked as night guards for their landlady and family. With time, some of Teddy's brothers had to leave their parents and birth land to start their own lives and livelihood elsewhere in other places.

Teddy was now left with only two brothers, Lobby and Fiddy. Lobby was a handsome one. He was also special due to the fact that he was a reincarnated uncle and showed additional signs of toughness and fierceness from youth.

When Teddy was no more of a dependable age on his parents and guardians, I picked him. I simply had no choice. Lobby was so beloved that he could not be parted from the house and family, some plans had been made for Fiddy, so Teddy was left. He seemed the least promising of the three: of a quiet disposition. He didn't like playing too hard and shied away from wrestling bouts and tournaments. His mother loved him. I grew to love him too, especially when I realised that he would come to live with me one day and I would have to bring him up.

His parents were good, faithful and loyal. They had served my family for at least eight years. They were simple and humble. They knew and accepted their lot and position in our compound. The relief of Teddy going away was evident on his mother. Having all her kids pestering her made her lean and less lively. She had to supplement their feeding occasionally.

Kizzy and Zambesi were not being paid for their services in terms of money. We gave them free accommodation, clothing and food. Their health was guaranteed and the safety and upkeeping of their kids were insured. That was the agreement. It was fine and worked well with no discord.

I had given this youngster his name "Teddy". He was plump, hairy and rather roundish in his early youth. He reminded one of a little teddy bear. He wasn't fond of me at home until he came to live with me. He was still very young and needed all the protection and care. He also needed to be educated.

I left with Teddy from Ibadan to Onitsha one day at 5:30 am. It was his first time in a motor vehicle and he was road sick initially and even frightened. But before the journey was over, he had got used to it. I had brought some meat for our journey. By the time we got to Onitsha, our journey had hardly begun. We were still to head for Makurdi and the time was already noon. Onitsha Township is a mad place. It is in Onitsha Market that you can buy something only to get halfway your destination and realise that you have been duped. In the Onitsha Car Park, stories are told of how travellers lose boxes and suitcases to young urchins who under the guise of trying to help travellers with their numerous luggage would disappear with them.

In view of these things which I had heard about Onitsha Car Park, I was very alert and cautious. I had a lot of luggage, and so I gratefully offered them to one of those urchins to carry for me in a wheelbarrow. With one hand clutching the purse and the other gripping Teddy, I trudged on closely on the urchin. Teddy was looking wretched and felt frightened of the crowd and din, and he attracted people to himself. They laughed at him and called him and me names. These were not strange to me as this was the usual behaviour of drivers and garage boys at all car parks.

As it was my first trip from Ibadan to Makurdi, I had not known that it was possible to get a saloon taxi car straight to Makurdi. Instead, I prolonged our journey by going in a *Danfo* bus from Onitsha which did not leave immediately until almost two hours later. I was very frustrated and worried. I wasn't sure of the safety of the journey or Teddy or myself. I was the only female passenger.

The others all around seemed to speak the same language. The bus was half-loaded with kola nuts, so that it was just Teddy, two male passengers, the driver, the conductor and I that were undertaking the journey. I started blaming myself for taking this route to Makurdi. I should have known better. Perhaps these people might take me elsewhere, steal my luggage, steal Teddy, rape me and desert me!

I was tired. I had almost travelled the length and breadth of the park to find this bus going to Makurdi. I was told it was the last. They lied to me by not telling me of the saloon taxis as I learnt later.

It was getting to 2 pm. The driver seemed to be waiting deliberately as if to start late, so that darkness would catch us on the road. Then Teddy started getting wild at those who were trying to tease us. This scared them off. I was so touched that I started to cry. He was proving he was his father's son. After some desperate prayers to God, we got to Makurdi at 8 pm.

Teddy was near fainting. It was now my sole aim to give him cold water to drink. When I reached my new institution, where I was to teach, I gave Teddy water while I packed and settled in.

Teddy was tearful and confused for the first weeks in the new environment. I knew he was missing home and his family. I devoted time to Teddy. He had his regular meals daily which was rare at home. His diet was rich. He ate what I ate and when I ate. He had his own bed, plates and cup. I could see he was proud of his new property. He even had a towel, his own special bathing soap, soap dish and a neck chain. All these were rare at home in Ibadan.

We strolled round about the town in the evenings together. When we did not, we played games in the field or played with our neighbours' children. Everybody loved Teddy. He was special. Everybody got to know of his presence. They asked of his background and parenthood which I supplied proudly.

He became even plump, radiant and lovely in looks. His teeth were as white as snow, even though his father's were of a very poor set. He was intelligent and was picking up the English language very fast. At a tender age, he was already showing that he would follow his father's career.

I got him inoculated against diseases of his kind. When I travelled out, I left him with a friend. There was the day I travelled out to Kaltungo in Bauchi by train. The parting scene was terrible. He had to be tied down. He didn't want me to go. I was all he knew and that mattered in this hostile and unfriendly world. He wept so.

Throughout my journey, he was on my mind. When I came back a week later, he received me so warmly that everybody was stunned. He was so excited; he jumped on me and hopped on all the chairs. He even ran round the whole of my friend's parlour twice. At last, I took him home.

His nickname was "Teddy Boy". The whole neighbourhood knew this. By now, he was already doing his father's job for me even though fairly young. It was with great pains I turned him out of the house to begin the night watch duty, and he did it so well. I was so secure. Whilst people complained of theft cases in Makurdi, my neighbourhood never did.

He was a playful chap and very friendly. He loved little babies and children between the ages of a year to seven. He played with them as he would with his brothers at home. I bathed him twice a week. He never enjoyed or liked taking his baths.

As Teddy grew older and bigger, the kids got scared of him. He became lonely and stayed indoors with me. He always sought for my attention, but then, I was a busy teacher.

One minute, he would tug at my bedsheet, make some cooing sounds, force a yawn—all to attract my attention and take him out for a walk or a game. Sometimes, I did, at other times, I didn't either because of my moods or some interesting novel which I couldn't care to divorce for Teddy's sake.

I remember one of such days when he was still much younger. I went to the bathroom leaving my novel on the bed. Teddy, in my absence, reached up to the bed and tore out some pages and ran out to play. I nearly killed him, using his belt to whip him. Sometimes he got destructive. He spoilt my slippers and floor mat, but with some harsh words, he stopped these. With time, he became well-disciplined. He knew how to behave when we went out to visit my friends. When I went to work, he kept the house. He was neat and didn't make the house untidy. After a bath, he managed to keep himself clean for at least two days. He never for once messed up the house during the day or at night. He kept unwanted visitors at bay. He made me popular having his rare kind amongst my Makurdi folks.

It was now early December. I was thinking of going home to Ibadan for the Christmas. Most of my friends wanted Ṭeddy Boy to spend the Christmas with them, but I refused. He had to come to see his family and our home again before it was too late. Either due to envy, jealousy or even refusal to recognise, his family might grow cold towards him if he didn't go home once in a while to see them.

So I left Makurdi with Teddy on a December morning, and that was his final backing on the town. We arrived in Ibadan by 6 pm. We were both welcomed by all. But it was Teddy's growth and appearance that surprised all. He was by now bigger than his brother Lobby and now more handsome.

Fiddy his other brother had, by now, long gone to live somewhere else.

His family was slightly jealous of him for a while and even a bit hostile to me initially. But after two days, all was well as I treated them all in the same way. Teddy and Lobby got on well, and his parents got to love and appreciate him too. Everybody at home and around all got to love him.

But one thing happened. Teddy was used to extreme good feeding, shelter, love, games, strolls and devoted attention from me. All these were robbed off him. He tried to seek my company as it was in Makurdi, but I ignored him. I had my own plans. I even kept travelling out of Ibadan continually.

Teddy stopped eating well. He started losing weight and became dull. I became worried and alarmed. My own family convinced me that he would get better and that it was all probably due to the change of scene and environment. So I calmed down.

Then I was to travel to Ile-Ife for a second time to see friends. It was the 21st of December. As I was packing, Teddy came upstairs to my own room. He had never attempted or done so since our arrival from Makurdi. I was surprised. He seemed sad and his sadness was contagious, but I couldn't place what was wrong.

'Teddy Boy, anything wrong?' I asked. 'Come on, say something. Surely, this is not you boy!' His poor feeding had not abated. I even had planned taking him with me to Ife. It would enable him see one of his brothers—Kinky. When I thought of the travelling inconveniencies, I changed my mind. Then, it was time for me to travel and without Teddy. My family all had to come out to hold Teddy and lock our gates so that I could go without Teddy who was trying to tear off from them and follow me.

That was the last time I saw that sad spark in his eyes and the life within his now frail body. He looked at me as if I was a traitor failing to protect him in his own hour of need. I entered a taxi and set off. I enjoyed myself at Ife, but as it was getting towards Christmas Day, I longed to go back to Ibadan to my family and to Teddy. I bought him a little Christmas gift at one of the Ife stores.

On December 25th, I arrived at my home at 9 am. I had left Ife at 7 am to enable me attend the Christmas service with my family at All Souls Church, Bodija, in Ibadan.

The house was full. My cousins from Lagos were around. Most of the members of my family were still locked up in their rooms trying to get prepared for the 10 am service. I greeted everybody. I saw Kizzy. I saw Zambesi. I saw Lobby. I saw my parents, brothers, sisters and cousins. They were all still excited about my arrival. Then I asked for Teddy. It was so apparent. The usual excited welcoming was missing. I asked again about Teddy from my young cousins, sisters and brothers. At last, I was told.

He was with his family outside our compound at 10 pm on night duty. He had ventured on to the road, of which he was not familiar, to search for the one who had even not cared to protect him in his hour of need. He had challenged the busy road, ignored the traffic and was blinded by the imminent danger he had placed himself. He was hit by a car.

The sound was heard even by the inmates of our house. The younger people in the house cried. The murderer disappeared. Teddy was buried where his grandparents had been buried at the back of our garages. Christmas was no longer the same. I couldn't go to church. I didn't want to believe. I appealed to my cousins and family to stop pulling my leg, but they were serious. I broke down.

They all had to go to church leaving me behind to mourn my loss alone, and I did it well. I felt satisfied. I remembered all our activities together at Makurdi: the pictures we had taken together; how he had brought life to me by making it happy and cheerful. So I wrote a long memoir as a memorial for him.

I came back to Makurdi alone. His eating plate became my candle plate and his towel my floor rag. Everybody asked me the dreadful question I didn't want to hear, 'Where is your dog?' I had to lie to them that he was at Ibadan.

His poem and story live. His photographs keep me happy. He will come back again, I know, and I will not fail in my duty again.

Chapter 2
Something Good

No speech or words are used… **Psalm19:3**

'Your heart beats fast. Are you afraid of something or what?' he playfully asked as he put his hand on her chest casually. How could she have had the heart to reply Eki without betraying what was in her mind? Her tongue was very heavy, but at last, she was able to lift her tongue.

'Eki, you are not far from the truth in detecting my perplexity.'

'Really? So something is the matter eh? Tell me, my girl. You have no cause for alarm. In fact, we've met barely three weeks, and all the way through, you've been a sweet and cooperative young girl.' After a pause of silence, he continued, 'I can't deny it, but I know I will miss you. That's why I want you to tell me your problems. Surely, I'll feel justified and satisfied that I at least did something for you, howbeit little.'

It was break time, and he had now formed the habit of sharing her break time. She seemed to enjoy and encourage it. They were standing unobserved behind the buildings. The matter lay heavily on her mind like the head of a grinding stone on its slab. It rolled over to the sides of her mind, while she was still not as yet capable of grasping the issue from a particular angle and presenting it in the lightest manner she would have liked to.

'I'm waiting, Lulu.' Eki's voice deep as an old gong failed to wake her up from her thoughts. The stillness of the atmosphere made the situation worse. Indeed, it seemed so contagious that Eki felt that if the girl beside him did not in the next two minutes release her burden on to him, he might be forced to shed a tear or two, and this would be very embarrassing for an average man of his calibre.

Looking at Lulu, he tried to probe the depths of the unknown mystery. As he pondered in his mind, the thought suddenly struck him that Lulu might just be feeling "parting-sick". But even then, this was natural, and besides, he himself felt it, and this surely could not be the whole core of the issue making Lulu depressed.

What was more, it was only three weeks of their meeting. He was a relation to Lulu's boss in the big city of Ife, and that was how they met. To make the ponderings of his thought more difficult was the fact that there had been no undue intimacy between them. They had all in the time of their interaction spoken of only things in general concerning work, the hazards of life, the political and social issues of the country and all other kinds of such chatting.

It was only in the last two days that they had brought their discussions a little bit closer and personal. Today was his last day with her and he would return to his own village at Modakeke. Yet all these discussions were in no way helpful in revealing what whirled in each other's mind. They discussed their hobbies, interesting debates, had arguments on things like where to lay the blame on between men or women as being the cause of miserable love lives.

Eki was very handsome, no doubt. His type of complexion was rare. It was clear. His inner body seen from under his open shirt was quite beautiful. He was amber shade like an anthill mixture of earth. His breath and body sweat were natural and pleasing. They always reminded Lulu of how a fruit grove smelled shortly after a rainfall. Or at other times, she sensed the incense of daisies in a meadow. His voice was deep and rich and his head ranked high amidst the general crowd.

Unfortunately, Eki was insensitive to the emotional feelings of women. He was never the keen type of man always expecting a turn up from acquaintances or mere casual relationships. He always spoke plainly on a topic and never outside it. It was no wonder he could not understand the perturbing anxieties of Lulu.

Lulu had grown accustomed to this handsome young man of twenty-five. She was a rather little person for her eighteen-year-old person. In contrast, she was dark, very hairy and soft-voiced with a rather short neck. She was plump, though endowed with an attractive figure. She yearned for Eki daily and prayed for the day something good might turn up from the relationship.

She wished Eki was more practical in nature. She had always tried to divert him from their common and general conversations but all to no avail. In fact, she was not even sure where exactly he lived or whether he worked or not and such personal data concerning Eki.

Eki could no longer bear the grudging silence which was engulfing them both with no fruits and he turned to her and held her closely as he would a junior sister.

'Lulu, you are not being fair to yourself or me either. What is a friend for if he or she can't share the problem of another?'

Lulu felt embarrassed, though it was wrapped in comfort, from the embrace and the thrilling feeling she felt from Eki. At last, she decided to leash out her burden to him.

'Eki dear, I have something good to tell you. But how will you take it from me? I love you very much.'

Eki was not immediately sure he heard her right, but he felt reluctant to beg her pardon. He had also realised he felt embarrassed and that her words needed a kind of prompt reaction. He was much aware that he was sending back a negative feedback by keeping quiet.

Meanwhile her head was sunk on his chest. He had a problem trying to keep the fast beats of his heart steady. This instead brought about a kind of irregular breathing pattern which he knew she could feel and he felt all the more embarrassed. At long last after a period of thirty seconds, he decided to react.

'Oh Lulu, it is really something good,' he heard himself. He had made the situation grave, more so as the girl was keeping passively quiet. He soon realised that his arm which were still under the involuntary act of embrace was now shaking and sweaty. He became aware of her femininity. Her perfume made him somewhat dreamy. He wanted to caress her, but he felt he would be vulgar. He wanted to keep on talking to soothe and calm her, but as he felt he had already blundered initially, he was at a loss of words.

After some fifteen seconds, something else happened. He wanted to scratch himself badly. He cursed the itch. He was too conscious of it, and so it mounted up to an irresistible urge. He had to scratch himself. He had not wanted to break the embrace deliberately for fear that Lulu might say other things, or he himself forced to do or say something he didn't want to. He felt stupid. Was he not a man of twenty-five?

At last, without any excuse, Eki suddenly removed one of his arms. It was the left arm which was in direct contact with the girl's body. He ought to have removed his right arm which was directly on top of the left arm on the girl's body. But then, it was the left arm which had an insect still stinging and sucking fat on him. The suddenness of his action gave a wrong notion to the girl because it was an action immediately after he had spoken. She thought he broke the embrace finally and she turned her back quickly on him.

Lulu felt ashamed and disappointed to start running off, so she began a very slow march hoping to be pulled back by him to make her feel that they were after all operating on the same wavelengths. He still did nothing. If he walked after her, what would he do? Embrace her again for an ambiguous while? If he called her, should he say something or what? Lie to her? No. That was not his kind of person. He wasn't in love with her. It had never even crossed his mind that she appealed to him or that he fancied her. She was more like a sister, nothing more.

The figure still moved on, lingeringly, unhalting but with faltered steps. He himself was waiting. No, she could not just walk away like that because he had merely wanted to scratch his arm. At least, she ought to turn and wish him good day or something. Should he call out and wish it to her first? No. He was the man. She should do it.

It wasn't Eki's fault. Lulu was a township girl. She was rather brazen but not haughty. Eki was the village man come to spend some time with his half-brother who was Lulu's boss in the town. He was not at all used to hearing a woman confess her feelings openly to a man in the way she did. He had of course heard of such things before but had never believed them possible. How can a woman do that unintentionally? If she did it, she was saying something else entirely, asking for something not immediately seen though not difficult to give. Her place was surely a brothel. Somehow, he couldn't place Lulu that way.

Then he saw something. A car was passing by and it slowed down towards Lulu's direction. She was now almost fifty yards away from him and was approaching the main road. He saw a man in the car tilt towards the opposite car door while the window automatically slid down. Lulu courteously bent down, and he could see her slip show from underneath her skirt. There was some communication which had not lasted longer than the flutter of an eyelid. The door was being opened for her, and as she sat herself in, she turned to face his direction.

He smiled guiltily, looking at her through a kind of invisible hazy mist his eyes must have produced to save himself from looking embarrassed and jealous. Where was she going? It was not closing time yet. She usually strolled home. She even sometimes asked him to go halfway with her as an excuse for an exercise that would do him good rather than sit all day at his brother's visitor's lounge, where they had met by chance. So rather than follow his relation, he would follow her.

His arm was then raised to wave a friendly bye. He knew he should not remain dumb. He must wish her a good night and probably add something else. He had no time to think to himself. As the car was now moving away, he stunned himself as he heard himself say loudly, 'Goodnight, Lulu. It is really something good.'

Chapter 3
The Rush

You will comfort me again... **Psalm 71:21b**

It started to rain. It rained everywhere. Nowhere was an exception. Even the intensity of the raindrops were evenly the same everywhere. The time was three in the morning. Many things were happening differently everywhere under the same dark dawn that was raining heavily everywhere. Some people were awoken by the rain. The lucky ones drew their blankets to their chins, rolled over and were lulled over to a sweet lullaby. The unlucky ones yawned several times endlessly thinking of the new day coming...

Some, again, thought of their unlucky conditions in life. Some others just stared blinking into empty space, listening to the rain sounds while time was slowly passing unconsciously. Those who happened to sleep in pairs, whether married or not, wrapped themselves soothingly and lovingly. Yet, there were some others, the heavy sleepers who knew nothing of what was going on outside. They would wake up in the morning and be surprised. There were yet some others who slept carelessly. Their pillows and cover cloths would be retrieved at different dislocated posts after the sleeper woke.

It continued to rain and rain, but the time was now 5:30 am. In many homes, life was already astir. Some housewives had started boiling water or trying to prepare meals for their husbands who had to leave home early. In some other homes, people were waiting for their usual time of 6 am before they could think of getting ready or prepared. Some others, especially the lazy ones, were beginning to think up the excuse they would have to say at work for coming late to their different places of work, as they felt that the sweet rain might not permit them to leave their beds voluntarily.

In Sobande Avenue, Oremeji, in Ibadan, the rain was no longer coming in torrents, but now, it was just drizzling. It was now 6 am. Bola knew that. No one needed to tell him or remind him. Something automatic was there to do that. It was his alarm clock. He had needed it so badly because he was a heavy sleeper. Sometimes, indeed, the alarm clock proved inadequate. Despite the rain, it had succeeded. Bola was a careless sleeper. When it had started to rain at 3 am, he was not aware. Like most young men, he slept with only a wrapper. After this, he was completely naked. As it had been an unusually hot day, Bola had kept the windows wide open.

Sometimes when the rain fell in the northern direction of the room, the rain water came through the windows and Bola had to shift his bed to some other safe corner of the room. Usually like everybody else, he knew it would rain on certain nights because of the weather signs. Sometimes however, there were no signs like this particular instance. Even if there had been any, Bola would not have been in the right position to know.

Bola, on this night, had his bed next to the window to enable him get whatever breeze was available. A crumpled weekend newspaper lay upturned with several of its pages fluttering about the room. It had been the paper he had used to fan himself before falling asleep. As he had not expected a rainfall that night, he became a victim to the very cold breeze.

He was unlucky. He could not, as a heavy sleeper, wake to readjust his sleeping cloth. His left leg hung knee-up on the bed, and the other was almost on its exit out of the bed. His lips parted a little making his mouth appear like an irregular hole. One of his hands happened to be between his hairy inner thighs. White scratches could be detected on his stomach and thighs as signs of an unconscious action of that hand. The other seemed to be pointing at his ears.

Bola was having a bad dream. He was tied up and put in a kind of big freezer. His feet wanted to twitch. Only the tail of his wrapper remained on the bed which was under his right foot. As the cold became extremely intense, Bola was now not too far from waking. He soon picked up his pillow from the floor and his sleeping cloth and unconsciously covered himself up while the pillow acted as another sleeping partner to warm him up. This was almost a regular pattern every night. He would never know that he did this.

He was soon fast asleep, and he saw himself in an expensive hotel. A beautiful lady was beside him, probably a supposed wife. They had just finished eating a very sumptuous meal. The waiter brought an incredible bill which Bola paid off as "chicken feed" and left a generous tip for the waiter that attended to them. He was dressed up in very expensive silk and cotton wears which indicated the kind of high-class job he had. The fat pipe in his mouth emitted out a bluish smoke as he spoke in deep, rich subdued tones to the beautiful woman.

At this point, the pillow slipped off to the extreme end of his bed, while his feet kicked it off later. Meanwhile, the wrapper was in its usual displaced post. The wind was now blowing a cold uncomfortable air, the rain having reduced considerably.

The woman was telling Bola how nice it would be for them both to go swimming later in the day and have a picnic. Then she started to laugh. Her voice rang out clear and loud disturbing the calmness of the afternoon. Bola swung his right arm quickly in an attempt to cover her mouth but found it hard, cold and almost painful…suddenly, he realised he was awake as he heard the last ringing sound of the alarm clock.

As usual, he had by habit tried to stop the alarm clock ringing and disturbing the neighbours. He was unhappy that it was already 6 am. The night had seemed so short. He started recalling some vivid pictures of his dream. The rain was falling softly, and he had to be at the office by 7 am. He was a clerk. He needed to be in the office early to open the office and clean out his boss' office.

Bola consoled himself that he could still have at least fifteen minutes more rest and still beat the traffic and all the morning preparations. Still contemplating on his previous dream, he dozed off.

A group of some excited primary school kids were speaking in the Yoruba language and calling more of their friends to see a naked man.

The bright daylight hit his eyes first. Then his consciousness was with him. He quickly drew down his curtain which in treachery had betrayed him. He had let it far too up to enable the breeze flow in smoothly.

He shouted to the kids to go away, 'You mannerless creatures, will you get lost?' But they had already picked their race on realising he was coming to.

The clock read 8 am! Impossible! He hurried up. He would have a bath when he came back. He pasted up quickly. He would have to eat at the office. He quickly put his head under the tap to enable him comb his hair. The din of the passing cars and people passing by was typical of that time in the morning when late employees were caught up in the holdup. He must hurry.

He rushed out to join the mad din and the rush of the outside world. Even as he left the Boys' Quarters which was his domain, he hardly noticed some of the girls still trying to giggle. He felt it was a pity that the quarters was too near the main road and that people used what could have been a sensible farm or garden as a footpath.

Just then, someone shouted, 'Mr Bola Whil!' It was Mr Yogbo who began to slow down on his bike. God was indeed kind. Mr Yogbo lifted Bola to Oke-Ado, and within ten minutes, they beat the traffic holdup.

Even before Bola had time to alight from the motorbike, he sensed something was wrong. Very soon he knew. Miss Idowu was asking why he was so late and that she thought latecomers to work should have enough time to take better care of their appearance. Then Bola remembered that he had forgotten to comb his hair. He heard the other employees heave a sigh of relief that he had come.

As Bola rushed off to apologise to his already fuming boss, he saw that all the other employees were outside waiting—some in groups, either inside a car or under some tree or leaning their backs against the doors. Then he saw Mrs Becky Johnson. She shouted roughly at him:

'*Jo* hurry up Mr Whil. I have some important documents to collect in my husband's office.'

All the other employees were obviously amused at his wet, uncombed hair. The trousers and shirt were all that of the previous day. One of his pockets jingling some coin-ish sounds was showing the dirty white of the inside trouser pocket.

Bola rushed off to the boss' office in the sole bid to open his door first. As he put his fingers confidently inside his trousers in search for the bunch of keys, he found only some coins and an opener inside the pocket. In his mind's eye, he could see the bunch of keys on his dirty, waxy table in his room far away at Sobande in Oremeji Area. Meanwhile, the angry voice of his boss with all the imminent impatience was hurrying him up. Becky called him all kinds of names. She also added that he deliberately wanted to ruin her life like his. He found himself stammering some inexplicable excuse that he had not brought the keys.

Mr Johnson, without any word to Bola, called his driver and Miss Idowu to accompany Bola to his residence for the keys and to should ensure he did not come back with them. He was being fired.

Bola tried to plead, but it was like trying to pour maize on the back of a calabash.

Chapter 4
The Fourth One

Beloved, let us love one another… **1John 4:7**

Emeje was a well-built man of thirty-five. He was ebony black. He was tall with a slight stoop and had a broad chest. Honestly, he looked very strong and promising as a man. His voice was one that marked him out clearly anywhere. Ladies loved to hear him. His voice made them lost in daydreams. As for his colleagues, they simply avoided getting him heated in any argument. His voice would drown theirs. It always seemed they could never convince their listeners against him.

He was popularly known as J.J. Though he came from Tarkum in Gongola State, he had lived extensively in Lagos, Ibadan and Enugu. He was the true Nigerian. He spoke Igbo, Hausa and Yoruba languages quite fluently which he used considerably well to his advantage. For instance, he never told people his full name. He would say, 'Just call me J.J,' with a deep grin that showed some false teeth. He had ended his matter.

He was now living presently at Ife. He was usually regarded as a Yoruba man. He mixed fairly well with people, and he was a very amicable person. He loved games, making friends, parties, politics and women. Yes, he loved women, and women loved him though he was incapable of retaining them. It was a pity. At thirty-five, he was single, divorced three times and with a male issue somewhere he felt only God knew. He always tried to reason out his faults and defects anytime he stood dressing at the mirror.

His first wife was Efua, a Ghanaian. There was no issue. It was the families that broke up their marriage. There was too much hostility and tribalism. It affected their love. It might have even affected their chance of having issues. He started behaving queer, and soon, he had to break up with her. Was he under a spell? Oh no! He was being too naïve to think like that. He was no more in love and did not want to continue with the intimate demands of a marriage.

There was Zainabu, his fellow Hausa woman. All went well for two years. She even bore him a son. Then all of a sudden, he realised that she was involved with another man and had been playing a double game. He got so mad that he refused to acknowledge their child as his, and so, she left. It was quite a legal divorce case. It was then he considered the business nature of his job unsuitable for taking care of a woman as properly as he wished, so he changed to the academic career as a senior lecturer in the University of Ife. It was there he met his third wife.

Susan was British and a part-time lecturer in the Music Department at Ife. She was a member of the staff club and loved playing games there. That was how they met. She kept pointing out his faults even in public, amidst his friends, family and colleagues. He felt very embarrassed. When he tried to hush down the habit and make her realise her place as a woman, Susan felt her freedom threatened. Then, there was this strange aspect of her as a woman. She kept on demanding those habits he hadn't quite assimilated into his intimate system like holding hands or being kissed intimately in public. He found her too forward. He didn't quite like the nature of her dressing, but this didn't bother him too much.

After some time, he started getting bothered about how she dressed and behaved like a man. In short, hardly had the eighth month passed after their marriage than Susan became involved with another senior lecturer in the History Department. This hurt him the most. They divorced.

J.J was a senior lecturer in the law faculty. It was Friday. He had just finished a lecture and was returning to his office when he met two lady students.

'Hullo babies,' he greeted warmly.

'Ah, Doctor J.J, good afternoon Sir,' one of them replied full of smiles as she tried to cling clumsily to the other as if she would fall. J.J was familiar with this fair, hairy girl in his faculty called Ladi. The other girl, Beadie, who was obviously the more attractive of the two, was only her friend. As J.J and Ladi were from the same town, he switched automatically to their native tongue Hausa. 'Hei, Ladi, I like this your friend. What is her name?'

'Sir, I will not tell you. You will not have the sweet eye for me any longer.'

'Heh, jealous woman! Doesn't your culture permit more than one of you? Come on!'

'Anyway, before I give you her name, what have you to offer me for the information?'

'I want the girl, not the name, and you will see your marks reaching the mountain peaks,' he teased. 'Anyway, I promise you something special. The girl is beautiful. You won't even introduce her, uncivilised woman.'

Their speaking in a foreign language did not in the slightest bit betray the subject of their conversation. Like a flash of lightening, Ladi turned apologetically to Beadie, who was a Bendelite from Ughelli, the Midwestern part of Nigeria.

'By the way, Beadie, please meet my brother. He is a senior lecturer here in the law department, the one I sometimes speak of. He lives at the staff quarters. He is Doctor Bala Emeje—the lonely one,' she added mischievously with a rich laughter.

Beadie who was normally a bit shy was hardly able to face him directly as she spoke slowly, 'Oh, I am pleased to meet you. Bridget Onah is the name.'

'I see,' said J.J looking furtively about the girl. 'Okay, let us all go for some snacks at the Accounts Restaurant.'

The distance which covered a two minutes' walk was occupied by a brief conversation between J.J and Beadie. J.J had gotten to know that she was staying at the same female hostel as Ladi. The same block but in room three while Ladi was in room six. She was a biochemistry student and would after the break at the restaurant be going for a practical lesson at the science laboratory from 2 pm to about 6 pm.

'Well,' boomed J.J in a voice almost too loud for their comfort, 'how about you girls coming to Oduduwa Hall to watch a play this evening? Do I pick you both at 7 pm? 7:30? Which is more convenient?'

Ladi knew instinctively the meaning of the invitation, so she had to give a false excuse that implied her being loaded with assignments to complete in the library. This way the invitation seemed casual. This also gave Beadie the opportunity to support her friend. She also added the fact that her course demanded so much attention and that she might therefore not be able to accept his kind invitation. J.J had to employ some of his male ego: the power of his voice, playing the dominant role.

'C'mon babies, all work and no play makes Beadie and Ladi dull. Hah, you girls, if you miss this play, you'll curse yourselves. Just give up two hours. If it is going to be more than that, I will release you and bring you back down. I promise.'

Having said this, the two girls had nothing else to say in defence, and so they succumbed to the invitation. J.J was to pick them both at 7:30 pm that evening.

J.J wished himself luck as he parked his Volvo car at the car park and walked past the Porter's Lodge into the female hostel. He tried to look casual. His friends had always told him that he often wore a serious look on his face, so he decided to keep his head downwards to the ground. The cologne he sprayed himself with whiffed all over him.

Inwardly, Beadie was pleased to follow this guy and her friend to the play. It would save her the fee of N2. She also did not feel particularly bad going out with a lecturer and a good looking one at that. After all, he was not in her own faculty, and he was a brother to her friend. She sensed he might take advantage of the situation as a man to get interested in her. This did not bother her because all she needed to tell him was that she was not interested. If this didn't satisfy him, she would have to tell him the common truth or lie as the case might be that she was already engaged. Beadie was disappointed when she got to Ladi's room only to find her totally in a different mood.

'Ladi love, *nawetin*?' she asked in the common pidgin language. 'Don't tell me you are going to the class after all.'

'Beadie my sister, I think you know Chris that my own lecturer friend in Sociology? Well, he says I should meet him at the car park where he'll pick up me up for a drive. In fact, I was hurrying up to come and tell you. *Sanu* my sister. J.J will do you good.'

'Then Ladi, I'm not going alone with him. I don't quite like the idea of being seeing with a lecturer at such a public place. If you come, people might understand and...'

She had to break off. Just then there was a knock on the door. Some other roommate in the room permitted the knocker to come in. It was J.J. He had gone to Beadie's room first and was told that she was in room six, and so there he was with all grins.

'Hullo babies, are we set? Or am I too early? Women usually waste a lot of time. But you both seem set. So...'

Before he could finish, Ladi explained in the vernacular the present situation of her not being able to come and Beadie not being able to make up her mind whether to go alone with him.

'I see,' he said seriously in English. 'I know Beadie would not disappoint me. Ladi, so you prefer the company of some other to your own brother? What a sister! Thanks to Chineke, I won't mourn. Beadie is here.'

Having heard him say all this, she felt unjustified and childish to back out. What was more, he was looking much more presentable than he was that afternoon. She had a soft spot for matured men. She was already imagining his firm and strong embrace. Resolved at last, she slyly tugged at her friend's neck in a manner symbolising to Ladi that, 'Well, it's up to you. We are off.'

After what sounded like greetings to Beadie in Hausa Language, J.J and Beadie exited the room.

For something to say, J.J opened up conversation immediately after they had left Ladi.

'You know, I was scared finding you absent in your room just now. I had thought of how I would punish Ladi for her selfishness in allowing you to miss the beautiful play. It is titled, "The Vow". Have you watched it on TV or something?'

'No, Sir,' she replied truthfully.

'Do drop the "Sir" business. Just call me J.J please. I feel twenty years younger that way.'

The play was not as fantastic as J.J seemed to press so enthusiastically. During a blackout staged by the actors to enable them change costumes, J.J put one of his hands on Beadie's lap. Then he moved nearer and spoke softly almost into her face:

'You know baby, I can't believe you are in your third year. You look so young. How old are you?'

'Guess,' she answered back boldly.

'Eighteen,' he tried.

'Nooo.'

'Nineteen…nineteen-plus?' he ventured.

'No.'

'Please tell me because I don't think I can believe you once I go beyond twenty.'

'Twenty-one already,' she said.

'Good God!' he gasped quietly. 'You look three years younger your age. What luck!'

'Why do you always try to sound as if you are as old as my grandfather? I know you are not more than thirty,' she countered.

'Plus five,' he said. Then he laughed.

She also laughed but in a way to demonstrate that she did not believe him. This time the play was on again but they continued their discussions in low conversations.

'Anyhow, you are a sweet baby.' As he said this, he removed his hand from her thigh and squeezed her left palm lightly.

'I feel lucky having met you. How about you? How do you feel?'

She had taken in his Dubonnet breath. It was intoxicating, and she felt a deep feeling inside the pit of her stomach trying to mount.

'Oh, well, maybe I feel the same way too,' she said carelessly. She did not care how he interpreted her. As far as she was concerned, if things were getting out of hand, she would put him in his right place.

'Maybe,' he mimicked after her. 'Are you not sure?'

She did not answer him but laughed. And my!!! The laughter did sound coyish from her to J.J. *What a sweet girl,* he thought.

No doubt Beadie was a beauty. She fitted in to any man's taste. Even women admired her. She had a smooth and clear complexion. She had white teeth with a narrow gap in the upper and lower teeth. She had natural black ebony hair which showed signs of recent perming. The hair was woven with beads, and it fitted her splendidly. Her breasts were full and supple. She was also quite fleshy at the backside. Her slim waist demonstrated this clearly. She stood not quite too tall with a long neck.

Her supposed boyfriend, Ikhide, was studying law at the University of Benin and was a fellow Bendelite. She was a bit reserved in nature. After the play, he drove her back straight to the female hostel. At the car park, he tried to retain her a little longer.

'Beadie, how do you hope to spend this coming beautiful weekend? Can I include myself in your plans?'

She almost gave him a fright as she replied in Pidgin English, 'Oh! You want to kill me. *It is acada for me, unless, man go* quench!'

'How?' he challenged back. 'After all, most of your lecturers are my good friends. I will tell them to be lenient with you. They can also lend out their books to you at random, and you would be able to take your difficult problems to them. I will let them know you are also my sister. Aren't you?' he asked smiling intimately.

'Well, yes.' At least to her that was a better relationship than what she had feared was on his mind.

'Okay then,' he continued, 'would you like to know my place in case you need to do some washing or cooking anytime you are chanced?'

She paused for a while before answering, 'That's okay. I believe Ladi too is free to come too.'

'See the baby again,' he reproached gently and quietly.

'Would I eat you? Why not try to trust me? I have some pets, indoor games, novels, albums and all the titbits you women like. It's a matter of a few minutes. In fact, Ladi already knows my place,' he added untruthfully, 'so pick the time.'

'Anytime,' she responded quickly and uninterestingly.

'Okay, do I come at 8:30 pm?'

'That's all right,' she said with feigned interest.

It was a distressed J.J coming out of the females' hostel the following day, Saturday, at 9:30 pm. He had not met both girls in. He was particularly distressed about Beadie who had not taken him serious. He recounted all the preparations he had made in his place a wasted effort, and he felt further frustrated. He had spent an extra hour in Beadie's room in the hope that she might return. On Sunday, the same thing happened. He felt defeated and realised that the girl was dodging him. Why didn't she like him too? He felt helpless. This time, he dropped an accusing note for Beadie telling her that she had spoiled his weekend most drastically. Then he dropped a note for Ladi requesting her to see him anytime she could in his office on Monday.

On Monday, the two girls set off together for the lecture rooms' premises. Each had a lecture that morning by 10 am, but Ladi's lecture did not hold. She seized the opportunity to visit J.J who was waiting patiently in his office. His face beamed up as he saw her.

'Don't talk to me,' he began in Hausa. 'You have seriously offended me. Ladi, why can't you try to make my case with your friend? Why now?'

'Doctor J.J, it is not that easy. It is true we are good friends, but there is a limit Allah. If I talk to her, she would see it as a calculated move to lure her to you. You don't know women. It might break our friendship. She might feel too proud to befriend you because of me or she might just take offence. Simply, this is the truth.'

'Okay, okay,' he said, as he softened down, 'just tell her we met in the bookshop and that I plan to see her this evening.'

'Okay. That's all right. Let me go for my next hour lesson.'

'Let me drop you.'

'No, don't worry. I prefer to stroll up. Besides, I'll lose some weight that way.'

With this, she went off. She was secretly hoping the match would strike. After all, she too was involved with a lecturer in Sociology. They would now both be sisters in "crime".

True to his words, J.J called at Beadie at exactly 8 pm. He was happy to hear her voice as it was she who had asked the knocker in. His happiness fused out when he soon realised that she looked ready for bed.

'Hi, my Beadie, I guessed something might have been wrong with you throughout the weekend, so I decided to check up on you. Did Ladi tell you I met her briefly today?' He bombarded her with questions since he realised that she was either trying to pretend to sleep or show him that his presence at the moment was undesirable.

'Oh, yes,' she said slowly in answer to both questions. 'Please sit down. How are you today?'

'Oh, very fine. Thank you.'

'As for me, I feel a bit cold.'

'Well, since I am here, I hope to shake it off,' he said mischievously. She ignored the obvious humour deliberately.

'In fact, I should have been asleep by now. I had to fetch water against tomorrow.'

'Can you dress up and come for some suya and something hot to drink to shake off your cold at the Staff Club?' he asked without hope.

'Oh, thank you. I feel too lazy and tired.'

'Can I help you then? It will do you good. Won't you even try to make up for your put up over the weekend?'

That was how he managed to pull her out of bed. She convinced and consoled herself that it was not a bad idea altogether to go in for some snacks and drinks. She must, as a matter of fact, be back by 9 pm latest.

On the way, J.J told her that he had noted that she was quite a reserved person and as such the Staff Club would be the wrong place for her. He would prefer they buy some things at the Maxi Supermarket and have them at his place. After this, he would drive her down. But Beadie was stubborn.

'Or,' she tried to suggest, 'I could take them straight away with me back to the hostel.'

'But Beadie,' he called in a voice like a dying man, 'all I want is your company for a few seconds only. Why not trust me for once? You don't seem to realise how much I adore you. Please Beadie. By 10 pm at most, you will be back.'

His house seemed to be just like the kind of person he was. Big, neat, well-furnished to fit his status and the whole place smelt perfumed. Surely, there was some artistic touch to be attributed to this man. The parlour, dining room and everywhere else were all lit up by a coloured bulb giving the whole place a dim glow. He soon set to play a record from one of Tony Wilson's albums. Then he proceeded to get the only photo album he had and placed it on her thighs as she sat down. Then he got two glasses and a bottle of St Raphaël's wine. Then he arranged the things he bought at the Maxi Supermarket neatly in saucers.

J.J served the two glasses and sat so close to her under the pretext of wanting to help with the pictures in the album. They kept on drinking and looking at the pictures for a while. By now, they had each drunk about three glasses of wine and eaten some meat pies. J.J picked her handbag and invaded its contents; makeup kit, some toilet roll, perfume and a purse. He opened the purse and saw a little amount of money.

'You are so rich!' he mocked.

She was silent. When J.J continued looking at her, she decided to take his mind off her.

'So where are your pets and the other things of interest?'

'Good God!' he exclaimed. 'Does it mean you don't find me interesting enough?'

'You are being funny. Shouldn't we be going now?' she asked trying to reassert her pride.

'Yes, I have gone into your heart. Shouldn't you come into mine? I am waiting hopefully,' he said tenderly.

She didn't answer him but proceeded to drink again. She had drunk most of the time as a need of something to occupy her, not particularly because she liked drinking.

There and then, Doctor Bala Emeje burst out his proposal and intentions seriously. He pleaded, discussed and talked a lot about his past life very impressively. She was still silent. At last, he became bold and embraced her. The new lovers became intimate for a few seconds. Then J.J continued his discussions.

'Darling, please let us make it together. Do you want me to be frustrated? Don't you realise how much I love you? Give me a chance my sweet one, a trial. Darling please…'

Though Bridget was touched, she kept on repeating that so well-known phrase, 'Give me time to think it over.'

'But darling, I don't want you to reject me. We must make it.'

47

'I know. Just give me time to think things over. Please J.J, don't rush me or I'll get confused.

Emeje and Bridget Onah went on beautifully together for a long time this way, and her love was able to mature. Ladi was not therefore surprised to learn that she would soon play the role of chief bridesmaid.

Both J.J and Beadie had become inseparable and were looking forward eagerly to the time all the ritual steps and ceremonies of marriage would be done with for good.

Chapter 5
The Obudu Cattle
Ranch Expedition

Oh Lord, Your greatness is seen in all the world! **Psalm 8:1**

It all started on a Friday afternoon, when at 2 pm, a man and a woman, as innocent as Adam and Eve were before their fall, decided to keep themselves happy companions by taking a trip to the Obudu Cattle Ranch in Cross Rivers State.

The car, a white Peugeot 305, carried its occupants smoothly and steadily. The car rode out of the premises of the School of Basic Studies and turned immediately left out of the compound into the road. The journey itself had not begun because the man had to drop off a friend at Vandeikya. After this, the journey then resumed. Vandeikya is the last town in Benue State before entering the borders of Cross Rivers State when leaving Makurdi.

The man, a true son of the soil and a Tiv by tribe, was by all means a true Nigerian. He came from the North Eastern part of the country, but he was flexible and broadminded. He was married with two kids and worked as the Assistant Rector at the Advanced Teachers' Training College, Makurdi. It was therefore not surprising to find that his companion, a spinster, working as a tutor at the School of Basic Studies was from the

Yoruba tribe in the Western part of the country. They had met during some conference during the course of that year by coincidence.

She preferred to call him Wanger, which was his surname. It was easier than his first name which was Tyorumun. He in turn, simply called her Fola. They both liked travelling and adventure in common. He had innocently told her of his intentions to look for curtain materials at Ogoja. It was rumoured that things were cheaper there. She had, with the same interest, agreed to accompany him if he did not mind. He did not mind at all, but he was not sure if he could make the trip in one day and hoped she would not mind. She did not mind at all. Though they had met by chance, they had grown a steady fondness for each other.

The smoothness and sudden broadness of the road told them that they had left the Benue State. In fact, the peculiar style and structure of the houses typified by their thatched roofs and mud walls had long been left behind. They both noted this with amusement. They did not rush straight into their intended mission of material buying, but instead, they explored some of the suburban towns of the state. When they reached a town they took to be Ogoja, they were disappointed at their discovery. Ogoja presented a different picture entirely from what they expected. They had expected a somewhat big modernised town where they could buy curtain materials. This had to be called off.

Unknown to both of them, they had explored the wrong place. What they thought was Ogoja was merely a village. They had followed the road maps wrongly. They then went to the township of Ikom but time being against them, the man reversed shortly before getting to Ikom and started for Obudu.

It was popularly known that there was comfortable accommodation to be offered there.

The time was 6 pm. They had both misjudged the distance of the town. They saw to their alarm that they still had an hour to make before they could truly be in Obudu Township. The alarm rose from the fact that they were in an unknown state that was hectic, busy and full of rogues. Anyone could molest them under the cover of darkness, and what an end to an adventure!

By seven, they were now on their way having been guided by some kind-hearted people who gave them directions leading to the Obudu Cattle Ranch. As the darkness wore on, it was soon discovered that the Peugeot 305 car had only one headlight which harassed their peaceful journey at certain intervals. Once, Wanger had thought the vehicle approaching him from the opposite end was just a mere two wheeled vehicle, but suddenly, he found to his alarm that it was another vehicle. Then there was this other instance when he had nearly run his beautiful car into a police checking post which he had mistakenly taken for an approaching vehicle. Luckily, being a skilled driver, he had made the best of both situations thus instilling his companion's confidence in his driving.

His female companion, Fola, had no idea about their destination. She had never known such a place existed and had no idea about the geography and history of the place, though she might have known had she been interested in current affairs. For instance, she would have known that the Obudu Cattle Ranch was an approved international site for tourists by the International Tourists Association. Also, she should have known that their president had himself made a notable visit to the place for a whole week. All this, her companion revealed to her as she listened with amazement.

They had about ninety kilometres to go. Already, it was nightfall, and this prevented them from making a view of the landscape. But the irregular movements of the car told them enough. The journey was an ascent to the summit of a high mountain. This was where the Cattle Ranch was situated. The road itself was like the movement of a snake, twisting this way, going straight that way, or going down the other way. Sometimes the road was just big enough for the 305 only. At other times, it could take something more.

Instinctively, the travellers realised the sharp fall of the temperature. It had become cold but not chilly enough to dampen their moods. The car had all its windows wound up to shut off the cold wind. The man was all comments. He felt exhilarated. The car's movement on the twisting road was exciting; something new and something to add to his personal ego and pride, that he was more than a skilful driver. The woman, by contrast, felt indifferent to his emotional experience and feelings. She neither understood the art of driving, nor the kind of feeling he was experiencing, what with the cold eating into her skin, the darkness around and the prospective gloom of the outcome of the journey.

Not that Fola was timid. She, in fact, did not mind night travelling, but then, this was different. She had never been there. Wanger had also admitted that he had never been there himself. The most disturbing aspect of it all was the fact that their car had been the only vehicle going in that direction for some long time now. This was not in any way encouraging at all. Very soon, they were at the peak, the summit of the mountain itself. The road signals told them they were there.

They simultaneously felt happy when they saw a "dish and spoon" signal indicating a meal for their starved stomachs since they had had no food since morning.

At last, they got into the reception. The route, the trees, gravel, stone and grass decorations were in themselves very impressive—a masterpiece of artistic decoration. They both felt transported into some other world but certainly not in Africa. At last, Wanger settled their lodging and feeding bill. The houses and chaplets were all in the Colonial European fashion. Chimney tops on top of the roofs, room heaters in the parlour and the way the rooms adjourned into each other was peculiar.

After a good supper, the travellers relaxed a little in the sitting room watching a television set showing blurred pictures. They were therefore forced to retire into bed after some conversation. It was a single chalet which had cost Wanger N80 for that single night! There were two beds. Because of the cold, the man decided not to waste his warmth alone. So they slept together and tasted the forbidden fruit.

Saturday, the following day, corrected all their errors of the previous day. After a good breakfast, they explored the pig and cattle farms. They saw the animal's sick bay, bathroom, and isolation room for those that suffered from contagious diseases, the food store and the resting ground. It was all like a kind of hostel for the animals. Fola noted the peculiarity of the pigs' eyes and likened their colouration to that owned by white people.

The next item on the agenda was the water falls. It was so exciting to discover that the Cattle Ranch offered its visitors several places of notable interest. Wanger headed off straight to the waterfalls and realised at a certain point that he had to abandon his car and make the rest of the search on foot. They both got down and hand in hand, chatting all the way, they did not realise the distance they had covered. Then they saw a vehicle in the distance further up the mountain fields and made for it. To their amazement, they saw two white men who had camped themselves there overnight. These two men had checked in about the same time as Wagner and Fola on the previous night. One wondered when they had found the time to get there and start digging the hard ground to fix their tents. These men told them that the waterfalls was quite a distance to make on foot and so they turned back. Luckily, they were able to observe the waterfalls at some other angle.

The beauty of the mountainous area captivated their visions. It was unbelievable that they were still in their own country. If they had seen what they saw in a Western film, they would never have guessed that such a picture was taken in their own country. As they drove carefully back to the Ranch hostel, they further discussed the nature of the white man and their advancement in technology. The Cattle Ranch was built by them during the colonial era. Their probing into the unknown, their zeal and dangerous love for adventure at all costs and their bizarre boldness distinguished them from the black man. Imagine sleeping in the cold, lonely mountain tops and abandoning the cosy and warm comfort a beautifully well-made bed would offer!!! *Funny,* they thought. *Whites were simply funny.*

The next adventure was the horse riding which was specially the burning desire of Fola. Wanger was not interested at all. He simply could not trust the animal. Fola did a little trotting up and down with the stubborn 14-year-old horse that pretended he was too old to understand or remember the signals demanding him to gallop at a faster rate.

After a few photographs taken with a few friends they had met there, the travellers decided to round up and quit the ranch. There was so much to offer. It was tempting. It was then that they observed for the first time the extreme beauty of the road—twisting, zigzagging, bending, curving, straightening, ascending, descending, rolling, unrolling, sloping…

Chapter 6
The Visitor

Don't let my enemies triumph over me... **Psalm 25:2**

Though a big girl of twenty-four, Dinah was like a kid to her parents. She blamed her spinsterhood for this, but her friends told her that marriage would not have made any difference. The truth was that she was an only child to Rev Solomon and Rebecca Ogiefa from Benin City in Bendel State.

"Chief" as he was popularly referred to [due to his protruding tummy as a result of his love for consuming palm wine] was not as iron-fisted as his wife, who was a sewing mistress. He felt there were certain times in the life of a child when a father should make his influence known. This way, a child would appreciate and realise that a caring and loyal father existed. It was only in her primary school level that he had handled her with an iron hand due to her poor school work then. After that, he respected and accepted her as a grown-up individual.

Her mother was a different person entirely. Many a times, Dinah wondered how such a pair had become a match. It was ridiculous. Dinah had grown right under her mother's nose. By the time she began her secondary school career, she was already a ripe age of thirteen. Her mother knew every personal detail about her. One would have thought they would be close. Dinah was secretive. She had been brought up the harsh way. Her parents believed that an only child should be brought up the harsh way so as to remain unspoilt and disciplined.

Dinah looked back to those long years gone by when she dreaded hearing the voice of her parents indicating that they had returned from some outing. She also remembered her love for the hours of night and how she always felt sad at the quick arrival of dawn. There were even times as a child when she questioned her identity. Was she orphaned or what?

What she could not forget was the day she clocked thirteen years old. Her mother had called her to her room and asked her to shut the door quietly behind her. After that, her mother asked her to pull off her pants, lie on the bed and part her two legs wide apart so that the whole of her young body lay bare. She was a bit shy and embarrassed, but maybe she had managed to conceal this fact from her. Otherwise, she could have gotten the severe beating of her life.

Her mother proceeded to tell her that if she was to remain her daughter, she was to keep her body the way she saw it then—pure and intact. She then threatened that if she was not a virgin before her marriage, she would have her stripped and pepper would be poured into her private parts and eyes and her body disfigured with blade marks. Dinah took this all in. She had vowed she would be a virgin till the night of her wedding. She had seriously meant this.

Dinah, like most of her friends, had wanted to be well-familiarised with her country by spreading her educational heights round the various institutions of the country. As luck would not have it, her parents wanted her around. She did her primary, secondary, A-level and university education all in

Benin. Her parents had made her form the habit of writing regularly and visiting home every other weekend.

At the university level, Dinah had played a rare funny game with her mother. It had actually started from her secondary school days.

Rebecca: So Dinah you are home for the third term holidays? Are we still "intact"?

Dinah: Yes Mum! I'll be home for three good weeks. And Mum, you still ask such questions? Trust me! Why not come and take a look at it?

Rebecca: I am proud of you. That is not necessary because when such things happen, I usually know.

Indeed, Dinah was intact till her fourth year in the university. Even when it happened to Dinah, it was not deliberate. It just happened.

After the completion of her university education, her mother told her to be patient for the right man. She also added the fact that the good Lord sent loving men who were themselves intact to the girls who had endured all scourging and sweet temptations of the flesh. She pleaded with her daughter to bear it all and preserve herself. Dinah had in turn assured her mother to continue having implicit trust in her that she would never let her mother down. Thus the game went.

Dinah fought it out with her parents when she realised they wanted her to serve her National Youth Service Corps in Benin. They prayed fervently about it. They even tried to run about the whole place making the right connections to ensure their wishes. This time with luck on Dinah's side; she was able to tear off from her parents independently for the first time in her life. She was posted to Kano where she worked for the Nigerian Television Service, Kano.

Dinah was enjoying herself in Kano. There was no doubt about that. Even though an only child and daughter of a Reverend, she had not been brought up to adore money and a glamorous life. It was not an understatement to say that Dinah loved and enjoyed men. She was a beauty anyway. At twenty-four, she looked about nineteen. People found it extremely hard to accept her present status. She was dark and endowed with beautiful curves at the right places. She had a smooth, clear complexion that lent her a kind of youthful innocence. This had helped her a lot, especially with her mother. She wore her hair short. Perhaps this alone actually gave her the youthful expression. She also had such lovely eyes and an aquiline nose. Her beauty compelled her lovers to be extremely generous towards her.

Her corper apartment almost looked like that of a palace. It was rugged with carpets all over, a beautiful standing fan that had a light switch and a radio/television set combined. She also had a video set. Most of her friends loved watching films in her house. Then there was her beautiful fridge. She was really enjoying the youth service. It was a good thing she was miles away from home. The only thing that kept her in touch with her parents was letter writing. She had even begun to have less time for replying, and this gave them cause to worry. Already, she had toured the following states: Sokoto, Plateau, Kaduna, Bauchi, Benue, Gongola, Imo and Cross Rivers State. In two weeks' time, she was due to follow Dras, her Kaduna boyfriend, to Port Harcourt in Rivers State.

Dras who was her current boyfriend was quite well to do and was a very successful businessman. He was very possessive and the most generous of all Dinah's lovers. It was not that she was morally loose. She was just a victim to the male sex. She was frank and straightforward. She easily broke relationships, but very soon, her looks would throw in another admirer. She was not stingy with herself. Once she was in love, she loved. She seemed however to be lucky with Dras. Things seemed to click. Her only worry was that he was a Moslem. As a Christian, her parents might not encourage the match. He was Danjumo Rasheed. She shortened his name jointly to a romantic little one, Dras. Many a times, she went to Kaduna to spend some time with him. He also came down quite often to stay with Dinah. To him, she was something valuable, precious and beautiful.

Then one day, something drastic happened which both of them knew that even to their dying day, they would never forget. The cause of it all arising from the fact that it had been over two months since Dinah last replied her parents' letters. In her last letter, she had expressed the wish to come home even for a brief moment, but the distance by road was too mind tasking. By flight, the cost was simply unthinkable. It would almost cost her the whole of her meagre allowance which was only N200. Not that she was in dire need of money; she simply did not see the logic for coming home and wasting N180 by flight or even more than that!!! No. They would soon see her at the end of the service which was four months away. Both Dras and Dinah took consolation from the fact that time flew faster than the fastest thing known.

Her parents had long replied encouraging her to come home since they would refund her the transport fare to and fro. Dras had sent N200 to her bank account twice now. Money wasn't really her problem. She would go later. She never quite brought herself to reply or to go either. It was the week she and Dras were to travel to Port Harcourt.

Three good weeks were spent in Port Harcourt. She had returned to Kano in order to receive her monthly allowance for that month. She had enjoyed a real good time with Dras. They had become inseparable. As if three weeks spent together in Port Harcourt were not enough, Dras came to spend the fourth week to complete the month at her end in Kano.

On a Wednesday morning, Dinah had a programme to record at the studio. By 8 am, she was all set, looking smart and attractive in tight-fitting native wears, and she was telling her sleepy Dras on the bed how to go about fixing his breakfast if she were to be back longer than 11 am. She told him she was leaving early so as to buy some stamps and get some other things from town. She had ended with a laugh saying how she could imagine her parents almost dead with grief. They had not heard from her for almost four months. On his own part, Dras felt she was the one spoiling them. It was high time she asserted her independence. He was particularly happy that she had not quite replied them for a long time, but he was to regret the thought.

Her parents were truly wrought with grief especially as their neighbours gossiped.

'That swine of a daughter. You know, now that she earns her own money, she ran away and hasn't ever come home,' said the gossip of a neighbour.

'Yes, it's a pity,' the other replied. 'The parents refused to be consoled or pacified.'

On that same Wednesday morning, the day Dinah went to the studio, the Chief sent Dinah's mother by the 9 o'clock flight from Benin to Lagos and then from Lagos to Kano. They had all the necessary information as to how to locate her.

Mrs Ogiefa strictly kept to the information their daughter had given them in her very first letter almost eight months ago. Dinah had never dreamt it possible or thought up the idea that either of her parents would ever dare to come to Kano to see her. How could they? Did they think Kano was Benin where they could look on her like a crop on the farm? But now, she was very wrong.

By 11:15 am, Dinah was back. She gave Dras a nice late breakfast of boiled yam. Since they were both alone by themselves, each wore only a wrapper next to their skins. Soon they would retire to bed to listen to music or to watch an x-rated film or anything else interesting.

Then tragedy struck. There are those times when one takes unnecessary precaution, but when the right time comes for taking the right precaution, it is not heeded. For instance, she rarely needed to take care about shutting the front door, which she did often. As luck would have it, things went on normally. But sometimes, things go the other way round. At about 12 noon, they were wrapped in each other's arms watching an x-rated film on the video television, when her mother finding the door unlocked opened it quietly. Oblivious to the lovers who were engrossed in their film watching, she stepped in. Then she walked into the adjoining room which was the bedroom in the hope of giving her daughter a big surprise and the joy of her life!!!

For the first ten seconds, it was as if those moments were taking place in dreamland. Dinah was too stunned to move or talk. As for Dras, he was speechless from shock and embarrassment. It didn't immediately occur to him that the intruder and visitor was Dinah's mother.

Dinah's mother broke the foreboding silence as she shouted in intervals, 'Dinah my baby… this is you. They have spoiled you and poisoned your mind… away from us. Oh, my enemies! What have I done?'

Her eyes were glassy. Her chest heaved in violent uncontrollable rhythms. Instead of bursting into great sobs as they expected, she swooned to the floor and fainted.

Chapter 7
Farewell

I will sing of the loving kindness… **Psalm 89:1**

I have always believed that love is something which exists as part and parcel of our lives. Every one of us, whatever and whoever we are, in our thoughts, actions, moods, expressions, in and at the back of our minds, at sleep, at work, at play and even when we are fighting, it is always just there. It makes its presence felt during those our unconscious aspects and activities of our lives. We feel it most when even the whole of nature and earth are all in positive tunes with ourselves.

We were a handy team of about twenty. Thirteen were males and the rest of us were females. We all hailed from different parts of the Nigerian Federation. We were at a humble epoch in our lives when we were to serve the nation in humility, so we bore all the travails and trials. We consoled ourselves that it was all for the sake of "service and humility". We, as a team, were assigned to make a fence for the motor park at Tyulen, a Tiv village in Benue State.

I remember the whole lot of us so well. Many of the men were clowns. They saw fun in everything and gave cause to laugh at every silly little thing. They made one realise that life was beautiful but something not permanent. It made one sad to think that part of life was meeting and parting. Honestly, they gave life to that company of ours. There were some others who were politicians. We enjoyed their rambling amongst themselves. They served as our News Broadcasting Service. Bless them. They kept us abreast with the rest of the world. There were yet some others who by the way they dressed, turned out generally or the way they played amongst themselves like small cowboys made it all quite amusing to watch them.

It was nice to sometimes feed the eyes with such rare sights and nurture some amusing thoughts in the mind. They did their own bit nevertheless. There were those who tried to be opportunists. They tried to see what they could get out of us seven females—some were successful, I dare say. It was all fun. I was the watching and observing eye.

The project was a month's business. We gathered daily at 8 am and set off together in a bus that could not quite manage our number. The journey to Tyulen which was forty minutes from Makurdi was always a cheerful one especially as there were various categories of people to entertain us with smiles, sighs and hearty laughter. We worked hard, cheerfully and diligently and rounded the day's work daily by noon.

Despite the communication gap between the villagers and us, we all got on well. They tried to help us. They provided water, gave us mangoes to crunch at our break and came to amuse us by saying some unintelligible things that didn't mean a thing to us. They came to praise and bless us. To them, we were something for them to watch with great pride and mixed feelings of pity and love. That the government had sent some people to fence their motor park!!! How kind. They tried to show their appreciation. We were each given some tubers of yams. Though I was looking forward to the close of the whole exercise, I remember how when the days were numbering near, I developed a queer feeling, *I would miss Tyulen*.

The villagers and their way of life reminded one of so many things that conjured up deep feelings and thoughts: their conical thatched roofs, the red earth mud walls with one tiny hole the length and breadth of a ruler serving as a window, the bamboo chairs and their own handmade toilets. The farms, domestic animals, kids and the smoking old people all made one realise that one was missing something inexplicable. The villagers were happy and content with their shares of lot from nature and life. I remember eating at a supposed "canteen". The meal, basically pounded yam with a native soup was very good. My tongue could not believe the taste. I remember the cold water from the big earthen pot and the goats and the fowls looking up to me from time to time.

At last, we finished our assignment. The fence was beautifully pleasant to look at from a close distance. We engraved in the cement our team of twenty for that epoch. The villagers were very happy. They got their spokesman to tell us that they wanted to give us a send-off party the following day which was on a Friday. Nobody quite expected much. The most we thought was a lengthy speech of thanks and gratitude by the village chief and maybe a couple of mangoes to buttress it all. We were to be very surprised for that occasion, and probably for the rest of our lives, to be stunned by what we all saw and felt that day at Tyulen.

Firstly, we were led past the various thatched huts that we knew so well to some other part of the village where there was a big room of cement make. It surprised us! One of the clowns claimed that the room was probably their chief's palace. Even at that, it was big, roomy and airy. The day had begun with an angry sun but somehow, something had appeased it as it calmed down and submitted to the winds to take over. We all sat down on three long benches with tables in front of us and surveyed the neat clean room. The village dignitaries themselves then arrived. There was a short introduction, a speech of thanks and gratitude packed with proverbs, praises and prayerful blessings. Then it was concluded with the hope that we would all enjoy the little of what they could afford us. He was greeted by a hearty applause from us. Then the most serious male in our team stood up to talk and thank the people on behalf of us all, stressing the fact that we little expected that much from them. Some prayerful words and praises were also returned and shed out on the villagers. The breeze blew in coolly, with a kind of aroma of its own making us all feel sober somewhat.

Soon after our spokesman had spoken, some damsels with real native beauty streamed in with all kinds of items. Bowls of water for washing hands were set down on the ground. Big bowls of pounded yam followed suit and were placed each one on a table. Then the soup followed. Calabash cups for drinking water were brought. The kegs of palm wine and *burukutu* were placed on the tables. As if that was not enough, bottles of beer, soft drinks and trays of fried goat meat followed. We were all very touched. The shy and surprised silly grins our faces wore, all told that. Their hospitality was too much. What really had we done? To think that some of their village youths had helped us at times. And what about those tubers of yams, mangoes and roasted yams they had offered us in sufficient quantity?

I simply had just wished I was in a position to throw bundles of fat money to them all, the way over joyous people did at certain social functions. But who was I or the rest of us? We all nodded our heads like lizards at irregular intervals to express how touched we were. Some of us who had sworn in our lives never to condescend to eat strange local meals at such places and from such people swallowed their oaths. We all ate to our satisfaction and theirs. The meal was very good. Hardly did we realise when the village dignitaries had left us youths to feel free and enjoy ourselves. After this, we took photographs with the village chief, dignitaries and some other people who had made themselves conspicuous and prominent during the course of the one month we worked there.

Then I was involved in a little "two-man" drama. An old woman seized and hugged me in great affection. I got someone to interpret all that she was saying, so we spoke through an interpreter. I reminded her of "a long dead daughter" of hers, she said. She prayed for me and wished me well. She was smoking and had only one upper tooth in her black gums. I wished her the same blessings and managed to offer her two Naira. It was like a hundred to her. Our clownish colleagues said that she was drunk. With a lot of hand waves and handshakes through a language unintelligible to us, but expressing farewell wishes and prayers, we parted from them. Our bus drove off with dust out of our handwork—The Tyulen Motor Park.

It wanted to rain from heaven. I was also conscious that my heart and eyes wanted to rain too. The cool breeze blowing into our rabbling excited lot in the bus, the blue sky, the palm trees, farms, goats, the old woman, the huts and everything else, I was backing away from them all at last. Finally, and forever. I would never have the cause to see them again and Tyulen. Our bus was going rather fast. The bus was noisy, but I was quiet and silent.

It was farewell.

Chapter 8
The Teacher

To those with insight, it is all clear... **Proverbs 8:9**

The classroom is comparable to the world, a small world of its own consisting of different kinds of people coming together to participate in a competitive game. Some are able to score while others cannot. Or it may be likened to a kind of race where some make the goal and others fail to. Then there is the lone figure, a kind of god who is responsible for how the race is run, an eye watching a drama. The pupils are the actors and the teacher the participating eye. As a god of his world, the teacher can make and unmake any of the participants or the whole actors as a whole.

At least in Karl's own view, this was how he saw the whole relationship between pupils and their tutors. Karl himself was a clown. He was a young bachelor. He loved life. He was a philosopher and approached life the way a philosopher did. In other words, the present world was to him the heaven itself. As a living person, he was entitled to face it that way, enjoy it to the fullest and seize whatever opportunity came his way. He saw his status and occupation as an escalator into life, fun, humour, pleasure and freedom.

He was aware that he was not bad looking. Even if he was, his position as an authority over some young inferior minds would scale away that fact. He lacked the admirable height women attributed as one of those qualities a guy should have. Then there was this curvy bushy eyebrow he had which hid his mischievous eyes. Those eyes were always smiling. He had never been known to show any seriousness or anger in those eyes. His lips were African all right, but they had a foreign quality in the way that the sides narrowed out considerably. This may be due to his fondness for drinking, piping and then most of all, excessive laughter which his mouth burst into quite frequently. He was also dark and hairy in an apish manner.

He was known as Karl. He even tolerated his pupils calling him that. He did not believe in manmade barricades or obstacles. He was a human being like his pupils were. They should, of course, call him by what he was labelled for identity purposes—Karl. Student or no, young or old, kin or no; it didn't bother him.

His students were principally females. They loved him, and he loved them too. He viewed them all as psychological actresses in his drama. They in turn saw him and his lessons as leisure—a time for relaxation. His lessons were the only ones in which none of the classroom cultures obtained. The pupils neither stood nor hushed down when he entered their classroom or left. On the contrary, the class was like a market square, full of rabbles. They hailed him in some by his name, others by the nickname they had created for him. He was nicknamed "OK". It was derived from one of his habitual mannerisms of speech. There was one thing good about him. He was devoted to them. He was punctual and never missed his lessons except, of course, when he had to do one of his pleasure trips. But then, he always warned them of such absence in advance.

His classroom was no better than Hyde Park. People spoke, laughed, commented, complained, or even became hysterical—as the case might be—freely, without any fear of opposition or contradiction. As usual, however, life is not equally fair to all. One man's honey is the other man's gall. His world was no exception. Not everybody enjoyed him or his lessons. But then, they were in the minority.

Yaw Karl was a twenty-six-year-old brilliant, intelligent, genius and a Ghanaian. His race did not prevent his colleagues from seeing him as a chubby pal. He was liked by all. He had a way of making people's lips go into smiles once they encountered him, whatever their moods. He taught English Language and English Literature. He spoke his own English with a kind of notable accent peculiar to Ghanaians as a whole. This always alone by itself amused his listeners. His business in that institution was part time. He was not really expected to undergo all the rigid norms the permanent staff was supposed to endure, and it suited him fine.

He drove a poor little Beetle car which told the whole world that its owner was careless, reckless and a miser. The car was worse-off than a third-hand rated car. People were not quite sure about the colour. People also wondered how he managed to drive in the rain. The absence of the left-hand wiper and the presence of a dead right-hand wiper called for consternation. His faulty silencer was like a loudspeaker. It announced his departures and arrivals as well as his movements. Being a passenger in his car was to feel more uncomfortable than pedestrians.

His dressing and general comportment told another tale. What did he do with all his earnings? Perhaps he was one of those victims of the usual traditional family circle. Perhaps he had a fleet of "poor" in-laws and kinsmen. But even then, he could have used some sense of "operation myself first". Most people in the school community, especially the students, could count his clothing and guess correctly as to what he would wear to school the next day. He was known in particular for his love for a pair of faded, old, not-too-clean jeans trousers which were neither white nor blue but more of an ash. Then there were his sleeveless shirts. Only the last two buttons were ever buttoned. The rest were usually missing or left undone as a matter of sheer habit. Perhaps he wore it that way to lay bare his hairy chest and an old tell-tale chain that he wore always round his neck. The four fingers of each hand, apart from his thumb, all wore rings looking like magician's rings. He just didn't give a damn.

His dressing all reflected his philosophy and freedom of choice in everything. His feet were always adorned with the Ghanaian traditional slippers. They looked like the Hausa leather slippers. His were black all over. No one could remember if he had ever worn shoes. If he did, it was a pair of dirty canvas that had no laces at all.

Karl brushed backwards his bushy black hair. He was always in the habit of scratching his hair. He never cared whether that left his hair looking unkempt. Of course, a wooden comb was always visible, sticking out from one of his trousers back torn pockets. During examinations, it was rumoured that he combed his hair in the classroom, which was actually undeniable. The best compliment offered on his physical features was his nose. Oh! It was simply lovely, nicely tipped. It really fitted him and made his face very unserious and youngish. None of the ideas sheltered under the umbrella of the traditional concept of a teacher could be detected in him. He was a person. Simple.

Most of his students enjoyed him probably as much as his colleagues did. His students were clerical students. They offered Arithmetic, Typing, Book and Account Keeping and English Language. He even taught them English Literature to boost up their standard in English which was considerably low. They were all trainee students in the Kaltungo Training Institute. Their standard of English always amused the clown of a teacher that he was whenever he was teaching. The way he taught and handled his pupils showed how sociable he was. None of his students were under fifteen years of age and some of them were married.

There were occasions when he asked a pupil to get up and tell him and the class what she did with herself very late at nights. His questions were always ambiguous and capable of being interpreted in many different ways. The particular student had seen through his joke and laughed coyly.

'Hauwa, are you there? Yes stand up and tell us what you do with yourself every night. Yes, tell us. Why are you laughing like that? So unlike your mates, you do not involve yourself in late night studies.'

'No.'

'What is "No"? Why didn't you say something then?'

The whole class all jeered at him, talking, muttering at the same time. They all knew what he actually meant. He also asked such questions to students who could not answer his questions correctly. He would ask them what occupied their minds or if they were not yet through with the sweet memories of the previous day. At other times, he would ask whether it was him they were thinking and dying of. The whole class would again go into another session of rabbling.

Unlike the other teachers, he never became angry with his students when they were late or had no textbook. He would turn the matter into humour. Sometimes the jokes were embarrassing. The women tried to avoid these situations. However, there was the instance of a rather pretty woman of twenty-two who came fifteen minutes late into his lesson. Her name was Nasare.

'Karl, good morning. How is your lesson going?' she greeted him with a smile and was making to proceed to her seat.

He simply said, 'We saw the "Daddy" that dropped you. Let us share the bread, Nasare. I am sure this evening is going to be a promising one for you, isn't it?'

The class all jeered in excitement. Nasare was embarrassed. She laughed falsely trying to defend herself but she was not heard in the din. It was even more embarrassing because Karl was at a vantage point where he could see passersby.

Once during his lesson, where it was obvious that certain students lacked the right text, he had reprimanded them as to what they did with the money their men friends gave them. The women laughed and protested that they had no men friends. Then he asked if they had friends. Some had answered in the positive taking the literal sense of what they thought he meant. Others were negative because they could not trust his meaning. He then announced himself as a friend and that if any of them needed the money in question for their texts, they were to see him at his residence at midnight, and he would

75

help them to it. The whole class laughed. They all knew what he meant. Though his jokes were crude, they knew he was not serious all the time. After all, there was no secret or open scandal as regards his dealings with any female student in an immoral way. He winked, dazed and looked at them all alike. There was no question of favouritism to anyone in particular.

It was his expressing and reflecting his philosophical attitude in practice into his teaching them that irritated them the most. It was the only thing that they had against him. They sometimes saw him as a person who was inconsiderate without feelings, or at other times that he was trying to show he was superior to them because he was a teacher. They could accept this attitude from others but not from him in particular because he had condescended to their level and they all saw themselves as equals.

He laughed at his pupils. After all, was he not a god? Was his classroom not his world? Was it not a drama where they were the actresses and he the watching eye? So he was free to laugh or even cry as the occasion might demand. His students, not even one, saw life in this way, not even the most brilliant and humorous of them all. When they failed or showed distress or blank stupidity in their expressions at his questions and made various English errors, he laughed at them. The most pathetic incidences were in their reading exercises. Here, even the most intelligent was exposed to his taunts. He was a terrible clown. When the students were desperate, embarrassed, frustrated and almost in tears, he seemed all the more amused. He enjoyed standing in front of a quiet confused class; all of them pondering for the right answer to his questions without a clue from anywhere.

He would study them all one by one, calling up the dull ones first so that they would attempt to blurt out the most ridiculous answers. Then he would weep with laughter. Though this was his custom, not one of the students had got used to him and the habit. He would drill them all on spellings, vocabulary and pronunciation exercises, but it all seemed for his own amusement. He was a sadist, a great one, a merciless one. He enjoyed and derived immense pleasure watching confusion playing on his student's minds and thoughts.

Then there were those words that sounded the same but were different in meanings and spellings—homonyms. If you were fooled by these, it was a drastic experience for you in Karl's classroom. He enjoyed embarrassing them and toying with their shallow knowledge. It was always worse not to attempt his questions because you automatically became a victim of one of his many pranks and jokes. Sometimes, these jokes got pretty expensive for the students. There were even occasions when the most humorous of them all could not afford to take his jokes. He enjoyed that too.

Tears, hisses, curses and rude protests against his behaviour meant nothing to him. Usually, it was worse off for such students who tried these gadgets as their defensive mechanisms to protect themselves from what they considered poisoned arrows. He would laugh them down such that it became infectious. This way, some others amongst themselves couldn't do otherwise than to laugh along with him. Yaw Karl was something else. Jesus wept!!!

The students were like cats. They knew he was the rat. Yet they could not catch him. They could not stop him and help themselves. They tried to enjoy and tolerate the most that they could. They loved him because he was not strict and severe.

Despite all his clownish performances, he was lenient with them. The weakest amongst them all, had always managed the borderline, and students liked this very much—a lenient teacher. If he was also to invigilate them for some exam in other subjects, he brought his pipe, comb and a *Mayfair* magazine and busied himself with these. When he caught glimpses of spies, he would laugh quietly to himself and continue with his projects.

Then it was one day for the cats. His students had not been able to tell him who an "African" was. He got all kinds of answers, suggestions, solutions and alternatives. One desperate woman, Asabe, tried to offer two solutions spontaneously in the hope that one might be right. She had said an "African" was the "dead ancestors". When she got the feedback that she was totally wrong, she added hopefully as a last resort to helplessness that, it was "a word referred to people who wrote books". It was at this point, he started to laugh so much. Then the most brilliant, Rahilia, tried to defy him by answering defiantly that an "African" was "a person, black in complexion". He had only pointed to a fair woman, Yeny, and laughed.

Then it happened. The students were the better for it. From excessive laughter, he choked and started to pollute the air. His coughs were violent fits. All the students quickly rallied round him to demonstrate their sympathies in one way or the other. He managed eventually to rush out of the class and go home. He wasn't seen for two days.

They missed him but not his lessons. It was an experience Yaw Karl was to remember forever. The students had all surrounded him patting him on the back, head, chest and even those forbidden parts—the whole forty of them. Not even one spared him, all saying and pronouncing "sorry sir" in different ways, "Shorry Shah", "Serry Sar", "Seorry Ser", "Suori Sia…"

Chapter 9
Tessy and Monday 8th

But those who trust in the Lord will find their strength
renewed... **Isaiah 40:31**

Monday 8th was one of those days Tessy Jooli could never
bring herself to forget. It was a day she now blessed when she
had cause to recollect and narrate the events. It brought untold
amusement. But then, when Monday 8th was still very much
alive on the calendar, she had cursed the day of her birth,
cursed her fate and had almost cursed her maker. Now that
Monday 8th was now past, it was a different tune. A very crazy
but blessed day.

Even on the eve of this day, she had noted with a taint of
sadness the fact that she was entering the new week during
her cycle. As a student, she loathed the idea very much. It
called for extreme caution, care and a kind of tension. How
about those premonitions, false feelings, faltering steps when
backing a crowd of people, or the high expectation of a call
from a fellow consoling female? Weekends were better. You
could relax in your room and have your rest, do things and
watch over yourself at your own pace and time. So this was
Miss Jooli's condition when she was entering the new week

of Monday 8th. She was three days advanced on this particular day.

She was a student of one of her country's universities, University of Ife, and she was in Mozambique Hall. Being in Mozambique Hall was a matter of "suffering and smiling". Indeed to school in this institution was to receive education with tears. It was a horrible mess engulfing everyone with mess. Miss Jooli really had it messy on this Monday 8th. She blamed certain factors: her maker, her fate and her date of birth.

She was awoken up early at 2 am, a time generally known as the "dead of night". She had a running stomach. She was in for it. If she had been at home, she probably would have enjoyed the ill-health of her stomach. She could even dose off while at it. She would enjoy the rumblings of her stomach and expect all of a sudden some squirting of the waterish foul liquid. But here was the very wrong place. No one ever hoped for such occasions. Even the over health-conscious students who advocated the need for the tummy to wash out its bowels at least thrice a week could not condone such a thing or hope for such moments. Her tummy did not rumble much nor give her so much discomfort. The feeling she had was that of immediate release such that she could not control her bowels. She was not alone in that four-bedded room. There were five others including herself. Having taken some tissue she thought sufficient enough, she proceeded to head for the toilet.

The toilets and bathrooms which were five in number faced each other in a large room adjoining their block. These were always filthy. The ground was all looking soddy with soap. There was stagnant water on the floor all filled with large green bottle flies having their baths, swimming, drowning or procreating. The ceilings were full of cobwebs and bee and wasp hives. The toilets harboured some choristers—the buzzing flies and mosquitoes having their fill and busy inside the bowls of the unflushable toilets. On immediate entry, you had to watch your head, feet and nose. Tessy waded in slowly like a duck as she took great care not to splash some of the filthy water from the floor on her beautiful legs and skin. She also kept a watchful eye on her person as she observed the moths, wasps and night insects all darting about and considering the intruder in to what they felt was their own bedroom. The major aim of Tessy was to detect the most suitable accommodation from any of the five toilets.

The first was a slap off straight away—too much stench even though its bowl was covered. That told enough. Even as she opened the door, she had to snort out. No one ever dared to uncover the veil of a covered toilet bowl. You might even see the incredible. The second toilet snubbed one—too many flies. What if they flew right into her body? The thought was too dreadful to be imagined. The third toilet sickened one outright and was a push-off even though it was a dance hall for the wriggling maggots. She was not going to provide them their partners and matchers. The fourth one suggested that whoever the last user was, she behaved like an animal. There was a lot of fresh matter on the floor which the co-operative flies were trying to clean up. As for the back of the toilet, there had been dumped some red cotton wool. The toilet bowl itself was full of matter and tissues. Hurrying to the fifth toilet, she had to shut the door. She had not been sure if she had seen a lizard or a rat. Ladies could be too petty about these things. A grasshopper alone could make many faint. A rat was unthinkable. She did not care to verify the actual occupant. It was already clear enough that it was not a fellow human that was in there. So she returned to the fourth which seemed the most tolerable of the lot. She cursed the fact that the halls lacked water supply and cursed the inefficiency of those supposed to maintain the place. After she had blasted her own contribution in to the toilet bowl, she realised that the tissue was not quite sufficient but she was consoled by the fact that it was soon going to be morning time when she could wash up herself.

Some ten minutes later on her creaky bed, there was further discomfort. It was from her stomach. It still wanted to blast and squirt out some more fluid. Tessy ignored it all. She would have to wait until she went to the school premises in the morning. Most of the school toilets were better. Some were sometimes quite good. She couldn't sleep for a long time and she was unhappy about that. She had an 8 o'clock lecture. It would mean she might feel dull or sleepy during the lesson. After sometime, her mind had stopped working.

It was already 7:30 am when Tessy Jooli woke up. That was rather a bit late. She had always needed all the time the world could afford her to bathe carefully, clothe herself and then finally make up. Now, she would have to look a bit like a nun this morning. She managed to round up at ten past eight. As it was a bit cold, she had considered using a shawl. Many things were on her mind. The most conscious fact she had on her mind was that she was already late and that every second was precious. She had even considered time insufficient to put her towel on the cloth line outside the room to dry. Instead, she unconsciously hung it around her neck thinking it to be the shawl and started rushing books into her bag and rushed out of the room.

It was at the Porters' Lodge that she met Rabi and Dama. They both had something to point out about her. In her haste, she had thought they were merely greeting her and criticising the way she hurried along. She entered a bus to catch up on time. She realised with indifference that some other girls were observing her. Even this was natural and usual amongst ladies. They looked at one another, sizing each other up, noting the makeup, shoes, clothing, nails, hair, handbag and what have you. In her own case, she was known for her makeup. Perhaps she was now looking so different, she felt a bit tingly. As the bus was about to round a bend between the health centre and the central café, thus approaching the second female hostel, the conductor began to call for fares and locations. There were some droppers for Moremi Hall. It was at this point, she examined her purse and realised that she had no coins. Rather than ask for ten kobo from somebody, she apologised and came down. She would rather walk the remaining distance which was a twelve minutes' walk. She might even stop by at Moremi toilets. They were better.

It was when she alighted from the bus that she received a mental shock as she discovered to her utter embarrassment that she was wearing her bathroom slippers and also that her shawl was her towel. There was no going back. She would have to stop by at Stella's room and take off the silly towel. Stella wasn't in so she hung her towel on her friend's chair and ravaged beneath the bed for anything looking like some decent slippers and left the room. A roommate was still laughing even after she went out. She had narrated briefly her tale of woe. The time was already 8:30 am. She still decided to go to the toilet. She would still go to the lecture no matter how late. Eddy, that bright guy she admired, was there anyway. He would explain it all to her and she would borrow his note and copy up.

Moremi Hall was much neater than Mozambique. Their water problem was not also that severe. Tessy was even lucky that the toilet maintainers were on their job. She went to a finished one that looked flushed and clean. She was however shocked to find a round worm inside it though she used it that way. She put the cotton wool barrier that lay between her body and pant on the empty toilet roll holder on the wall. She tried to force her tummy. It surprised her. She had nothing for the toilet. As there was not enough water to flush since it was still filling up slowly, she proceeded to open the door and go out. She did not have to feel too bad because she had only pissed. It seemed also that she and the cleaners were alone. However, when she came out, she felt a bit surprised to find another girl waiting to go in. They were somehow familiar with one another and so they greeted each other rather casually. Tessy had to clear herself.

'Oh,' she began, 'I found a worm there. It can't get flushed somehow,' she ended.

'It's one of those things one has to cope with,' said her listener. 'One has no choice.' With that, she parted.

As she was just about stepping out of the hostel, her heart stopped with a heavy thud for about three seconds. She was feeling incomplete and empty somewhere, and she knew where. Her cotton barrier was missing. Her immediate private body and undies were in close, intimate contact. It was all that she had. With that, she rushed back to the worm's toilet. The other girl had left. Her cotton barrier was still there.

Shrugging, she placed it back in place and continued on her way again. She felt bad and cursed her absentmindedness. The time was now about twenty to nine. If she were to make a straight head for the next lesson, she would be too early. It would mean loitering around as if she was too eager for a lesson of the next hour. This wasn't the case. Therefore she decided to go to the bukataria to have a quick meal of rice to kill the time a bit. She had now decided to go when the lesson was over so as to meet Eddy and his lesson notes.

The bukataria, popularly known as the "buka" by all the campus inmates, was another world of its own. There were mini shops of all kinds, various workshops of all kinds and various eating places of all kinds. All kinds of foodstuffs were cooked and sold. It took a regular customer to the buka to know the right places for the particular foodstuff. If you were the kind of person who loved peppery stuff, you had to know the right place. If you were the type of person who did not quite mind cold meals, you simply had to know where to get that medium. Again, if you were choosy about quantity rather than quality, it also took you to be a regular customer to the buka to know where to get your tastes. Within four minutes, Miss Jooli was seated at Iya Beta's inn. She was the quantity consumer kind of a customer. She did not particularly mind where she ate in so far as the meal was tasty and worth the amount she paid for. It was also an inn for people who did not mind the soups and sauces not tasting fresh. So she was in the right place.

After she filled a plastic old cup with water from an earthenware pot, she cleaned the bench and sat ready to begin elementary procedures on the meal which involved mixing and salting to taste. It was while she was engrossed in this that

86

some of the contents in the aluminium plate were involved in an accident. Her twenty kobo piece of meat with a few grains of stewed rice dropped to the floor. There weren't too many customers yet in the inn. Probably if she were sitting in some inconspicuous corner, she would have retrieved the piece of meat unobserved.

Most of the eating inns at the bukataria operated on a "pay before you eat" service. Others operated the other way round. If it happened that one was a regular customer, you were allowed to break regulations. Tessy was, by now, fed up with herself. Even though a well-known person at the inn, she was ready to pay up after the meal. Then she realised another mishap. Her purse was no longer in the bag. There!!! She had remembered. It was in Stella's room because it was empty after all. With obvious sincerity and apparent embarrassment, she was heard above the din of the smoky room apologising and explaining. She was quickly forgiven by the chef who assured her of her confidence and trust in her as a customer.

It was now five minutes to nine. She would just be in time to see her other mates coming out of the lecture room. She was lucky. She caught up with Eddy who gave her his lesson notes. There was another lesson they all had together by eleven, so she could return his notes then. She sat in the library and managed to copy the note.

When it was eleven, she was already at the venue of the lesson on psychology. She returned Eddy's notes and got settled. The lecturer came and gave his lesson while the students all recorded all he had said in their notebooks. Towards the end of the lesson, the lecturer made a necessary digression by referring to the previous lesson notes. It required the students to flip backwards their note leaves.

Everybody did. Tessy did too, but she was the only one confused and dismayed. She had unknowingly taken down the lesson into the wrong notebook. This meant extra work.

Immediately after the lecture, as all the students were leaving the room, Tessy Jooli suddenly became conscious of her having stained her clothes. Her uneasiness grew in to a nervous panic. Tessy Jooli was a shy, young nineteen-year old lady by nature. She was in her first year. She had a serious-looking, pretty face that gave people the impression that she was a snub. Unfortunately, she was not quite too friendly because she was shy. She did not go out of her way to make friends though she had quite a few acquaintances. With her male counterparts, that tendency was not there. Men were always easier and accessible as friends than the haughty women. She was at ease with men because they took the trouble to seek her friendship; and once that was settled, there was no longer any problem. Again, being a lovely girl that she was, she got herself attracted to them. Anyway, she was not prepared to commit herself to any permanent relationship.

When Eddy detected Tessy's wanting to stay back a little, he also decided to wait. He enjoyed helping her out with her academics difficulties. Tessy saw and realised the implication of what she was letting herself into, and therefore, she had to make as if all of a sudden, she had changed her mind. She then decided to do what Miss Joke Adelabu did: pretend, feel indifferent, and walk amidst the crowd without observing them. She was going to do just this, and with a help of a serious frown on her snobbish face, she would distract all unwanted attention. She did all the way to Moremi Hall successfully. She found out to her relief in the loo that she had overreacted. The undies, yes, but not the main garment. Why had she felt so strongly that way that she had soiled herself? She all of a sudden felt unwell and sick of the young day already. She made for Stella's room.

Stella was back. She told Tessy how the strange purse and towel had alarmed her. She had not seen any of her roommates to let out the cat out of the bag. Tessy incurred her sympathy by narrating the woeful events that had since befallen her. Tessy was also blaming the day of Monday. She said she had never liked Mondays. She could remember that it was on a Monday that she pulled out a molar.

Having been refreshed, Tessy left Mozambique Hall. She was looking her real self. Her feet were now adorned with beautiful black heeled shoes. She was elegant. Pity the whole of the morning crowd hadn't seen her this way. Many of them might not have cause to meet her again till the following day. She was going back to the buka to pay up her debt because she did not want to forget.

It was now about 2 o'clock in the afternoon. The sun was very hot. Many people were in the cafeteria or in their room having siesta. Many others too were in the bukataria, library or in the laboratory. Some lazy students stabbed out their lectures in preference to sleep or playing draught as the males would, or cooking as the females would. Everywhere seemed deserted and quiet. Only a few legs were moving around. Tessy's were among them. She was going to the bookshop. She was a lover of books. She had a fantastic collection of all kinds of books both at her home and in the hostel. She spotted out a book on Friday, and she was going now to buy it. It was this alone that had motivated her chance of paying up at the bukataria. The scourging sun in all its might had not been enough to dissuade her. She was perspiring from all her respiratory angles. She cursed the sun.

The bookshop joined the train of traitors. The book was no longer there. She even examined those sections of the bookshelf where it was impossible for the book to have been. Still, she was met with hard luck. She felt very defeated. To have come all the way from Moza Hostel under the sun to meet this! She took a bus back to the hostel. At the Porter's Lodge, the heel of one of her lovely shoes came off. She was very unhappy. It meant sparing some time and money for the cobblers. She looked into her own pigeonhole for her room. Every roommate had a letter. Some even had two. Miss Jooli had none. Not even a postcard. She loved writing and receiving letters.

Tessy was in the fourth room on Block Four. She normally said "four-four" to indicate her residence. In her absentmindedness, she entered the wrong room, apologised instantly and stepped out. She gave her excited roommates their letters and settled herself in the lower part of the bunk bed for siesta. It was about 4 pm. After some time, she realised the craving need of her tummy to release its bowels. She felt like crying. Why didn't the tummy feel this way while she was at the right places? As the urgency of her bowel increased, she realised she had no choice but to go to the toilet. If it were morning time, she could have counted herself lucky because the toilet bowls would have been cleaned by the maintainers. By now however, the bowls would have all been refilled. The floors were already flooded by those afternoon bath takers. She could picture it all too vividly. Her tummy rumbled on. There was a lot to be released. That she knew.

Miss Jooli could not bear to face the toilets she knew so well already. She'll rather go elsewhere. She hurriedly dressed up and a few minutes found her inside a bus that was to drop her at the school premises. It was quicker than being dropped at Moremi Junction and having to walk up the pathway to the hall. She also thought it a blessing that those town service buses came into circulate round their campus.

Tessy Jooli was in haste. Her control over her bowels was waning down considerably fast. There was no time to make a slow march the way ladies did on heels. The Students' Union Building was the first that one encountered when approaching the academic grounds. It was here she alighted to dart for the staircase leading to the upper base of the building. That was where parties and other social activities were in operation. She ran to the ladies'. There were three toilets in all. One was permanently locked. The second was under repairs and banned from temporary usage. The third was good, but right now it was occupied. Her feet were restless. They exchanged her weight in turns which made her seem to be rocking herself in a slow kind of jig. Her control was considerably weakened by now. She could feel her anus spitting out some of the fluid. When at last the occupant came out, she hardly noticed who and rushed in…

It was all very pathetic. Tessy Jooli was wasting her precious siesta hours. She had an evening lecture at 6 pm. She also had not had any meal apart from that which she had at around nine that morning, though this was usually her daily routine and she remained slim and lovely. Immediately, she sat herself on the toilet seat which she hadn't given enough time to clean up properly. Her tummy roared and almost immediately, her anus vomited like a tap at a go. She felt that calm eased relief after that kind of stomach disorder.

Back at the hostel again, she was considering her presence for the evening lesson. The decision was negative. She was not well. She would not go. She needed at least to eat, have an evening bath and rest or sleep. She would spend some of the night prep copying up notes. She did just these with no basic tragic interruption except for the little incidence in the bathroom. She had lost her bathing soap when it dropped on the bathroom's floor which was considered too unhygienic for one to retrieve anything, no matter how precious. Panties, brassieres, newly opened costly medicated soaps, handkerchiefs and cheap trinkets were usually surrendered to the pool. The only exceptions were money and gold items.

Miss Jooli was coming down from prep to the hostel premises with Stella Jaiyeoba. It was going to 11 pm. The night was rather warm. They strolled down the thirty minutes' walk to their rooms. But Stella had only to walk fifteen minutes since Moremi Hall was fifteen minutes away from where they had done their prep. The remaining fifteen minutes took Tessy down to Mozambique. She was ruminating in her mind how fast the day had been and the various ill lucks she had encountered. She was now thankful to her maker that the old always gave rise to the new. Mondays were the only days when she had early morning lectures. It was now 11:30 pm. Monday 8th was very old in time and ailing. There were only thirty minutes to see it out of the calendar forever. But what happened in the next few minutes showed that it still possessed some youthful vigour.

Tessy Jooli was ironing a pretty frock. It was what she did every night. She could not afford to rely on the electric supply for the new day. All of a sudden, she felt a slight vibration from the iron and assumed it was a shock. She left the hot iron abruptly and turned to express her new discovery about the iron to Morayo, her bunkmate. As they were discussing the sanity of the iron, there was a queer smell. Then they both instinctively knew what had happened. Monday 8th had burned up Miss Jooli's frock and she started to lament. The iron's face was badly charred but the worst was her sixty-five Naira dress. Even the most experts of tailors could never give the dress its right outlook. Tessy continued to lament. *O God! Why did you create Mondays? See all my trouble for today. God punish Monday…*

It was midnight; Morayo pulled out another frock and started to iron it. At least, that action and gesture began another day well.

Chapter 10
Flower in Winter

My salvation and honour depend on God… **Psalm 62:7**

When you looked at Martina Vande, you guessed immediately that God himself had it in mind to create a flower or that she was created on the completion of a flower. She was a colourful Nigerian. Her hair was ebony black even as the pupils of her eyes. The portion surrounding the pupils was sky blue, and when she smiled, she revealed a set of heavenly white teeth. Her complexion was yolk. She adorned her body always with colourful clothing. It was simply her style.

Martina was soft-hearted. Her heart was as soft as a petal could be. She was delicate and could easily be hurt. When she was hurt, her spirit crumpled. She was like pollen to the men of the world. Sometimes she was broken, crumpled, dashed to pieces and dropped to the ground as of no worth. Sometimes again, she was embraced, cherished and adored as a gem of worthy acquisition.

She didn't bloom all the time but had her seasons of change. It all depended on the forecast of the weather. When life itself became too hot, scorching and intolerable like a menacing sun, she became wilted and withdrawn. When the tune was otherwise, she became like a nipping bud, new, fresh, green and rich in foliage. She was at her best then. It was as if she had excess pollen grains to donate to every inhaler and sucker. When this did happen, she became like a dry twig in autumn, all its leaves stolen and shed off from it. She looked dry, bare and ugly then. She would need all the time and relaxation to bring her body back to spring.

Indeed, Doctor Yahaya was like a gardener to her. He always recommended vitalising capsules. Sometimes, he prescribed a timetable of rest and relaxation. Martina was only eighteen, young and colourful. Her beauty exposed her to the world and she was devoured. No matter where she stood and placed herself in the world, she was sighted, seared off from her stand and skinned again. It seemed an ever-scalding syrup of a cycle.

It all started when she met Yakubu Hassan. She was carried away by his flamboyant language as he took the robe of a poet and turned her into a poem. She would never forget the circumstances under which she had met him. She blamed herself for her uncontrollable emotions. It was enough for people to note her beauty and get attracted. Anything to add to that was magnetising people towards herself like the case of Yakubu.

Martina loved animals. She spent virtually all her time on certain Sundays in the zoo. She was a nursing student. She could not stand cruelty to animals. She was home on vacation from college, and she was going to the market when she noticed a scene she would have hated ever to see. There was a lot of commotion going on in a respectable-looking compound. Some decent and some not so decent people had gathered to constitute themselves as onlookers and observers. Martina Vande joined the crowd, and her emotions spilled out all over her. Many people saw her and Yakubu Hassan was among.

There was a female cow whose eyes already were very much dilated and red as if it were crying but no doubt due to fear. It was trying to challenge any of its attackers who all possessed massive ropes, logs of wood and leather whips. To Martina, the cow was crying. It was afraid. It didn't want to die. It was frightened to surrender. It could guess too well what those gadgets of brutality and death would be like on its tender hide. Her nose was running and she had her horns dangerously directed to any that dared to defy her courage. She probably had seen the fate of some other. Most of the onlookers were alert and cautious. It was rumoured amongst the crowd that she was a runaway cow on the loose. The poor cow was like a mouse who thought it was clever and had the chance of freedom at last while the cat seemed timid and tied.

Soon, her attackers made loop ropes, flung them round her neck and legs, and she was pulled roughly from different angles. Her eyes became larger as she clenched her teeth on her own tongue in agony. She was almost choking. She fell down roughly and painfully. There was a lot of triumphant noise from the crowd as they unleashed several hard slaps and blows on her sore, red hide with their whips and sticks. Each groan of the cow and each blow on it made Martina tremble and weep. All her body was clenched and tight, and there were goose pimples on her skin as if she were cold. She could not hide her anguish as she cursed out aloud to the brutes. One of them was putting his ugly, dirty, scarred leg on the cow's bony hip while another was pulling at its tail as if to uproot it from its socket. The cow was breathing fast and Martina Vande's tears flowed down fast.

Now that they had got it trapped, the men proceeded to drag the cow. Her skin was being peeled against the hard stony ground and eventually she was hurled into the back of a hired lorry with the men using such amazing strength. Some people were laughing at Martina. Someone made a cruel remark that she would soon come to buy the cow's meat to eat. Only Yakubu Hassan shared the same pathetic feelings with her. After a brief formal introduction, he offered to give her a treat at a restaurant, take her to the market and then take her back home. He was telling Martina how shocked he was to behold such a beauty weeping. That was how they became friends.

She had insisted on purchasing the items first at the market before going to the restaurant. He helped her with ten Naira and also hoped she wouldn't be long. She only had to buy two bars of key soap, so within ten minutes, she was back to the car with him. He drove off to a quiet little hotel where they spent some intimate moments. He was Fulani, fair and flexible. He melted her. He told her he wanted them to strike a meaningful relationship. He told her he would take her round the next day to meet some "big" people who would always help her out of any "Nigerian situation" that needed "long legs" to help her out of difficulties. She was also going to meet a friend of his who would readily give her the tickets to enable her visit him in Sokoto. He even said that was the first place they would go after leaving the hotel because he was due to travel back in a few days' time. He would want her to come and see how Sokoto looked like.

Yakubu Hassan manoeuvred and managed his tongue so well that Martina was carried off. Many things came into her mind. So, she was that pretty and lucky! She had fallen into that admirable group of ladies who got whatever they wanted in the world because of the kind of association they had with certain men. She saw a new caste in herself with good clothing, trinkets and a more promising life. However, she was going to be careful. A little pollination for a wee bit of nectar.

True to his words, the lovers went to some two places where he spoke his own dialect, since Martina was a Tiv, she would probably understand Hausa. He did not yet introduce her to anybody. He told her later that the right people were not the ones she saw and they would continue the tour of visits the next day. It was already very much past seven in the evening when Martina was dropped at her residence by Yakubu. That was the last she ever saw of him.

Martina felt bad after the episode. For a long time, she looked weather-beaten as she carried herself gloomily about. She returned to college still looking wilt and withdrawn. The fact kept dawning on her that she was virtually comparable to a harlot, maybe even worse. She had debased her precious body. What she considered highly dear and worth billions had been given off for ten Naira!!! But with time, she got over it because, after all, she had enjoyed the affair. She sometimes even thought of the occasion when she wanted to keep herself thrilled and excited. It was part of being a woman. You couldn't at all times twist a man.

Consoling herself with that, she bloomed again and put life in to her work. She was a first-year day student nurse at the School of Nursing, Makurdi. It was on a Saturday. She thanked God for that. What with having to get up early during the weekdays to continue the struggles of life and only to come back home and find domestic strings trying to tie one and choke the thread of life out of one. But with weekends, it was always different. The time was ten in the morning. She lay in bed like a curled up snake. Of course, she was wide awake but she just preferred staying up in bed, lying snug and warm and letting her imaginations run wild.

On Saturdays, there was usually all her dirty belongings to wash, her hair to plait, her room to tidy, the house to clean up, the dishes to wash, marketing and cooking. Most times, she was relieved of more than one of these. Thank God she shared from the benefits of the Nigerian extended family system. As she lay on her bed thinking of what she had to do, she felt very disconcerted and she rose up. By 3 pm, her own room looked inviting and her dirty belongings all looked attractively displayed under the sun's rays. Still, she had to go shopping where she met another agent of misery.

The Wadata Market in Makurdi is most unique. From whichever angle you approached it, the beautiful view of the Benue River came up. The market itself was most popular. It was the main market of the town for the people. One usually found whatever one wanted there. It was a market constituting various sections and lanes for different goods, items, stuffs and wares. The traders too were mostly Easterners. They made one feel amused shopping at the market.

Martina soon stepped into the market. She wanted to buy meat and many other things. As she made her way into the meat stalls, her steps were obstructed by some of the overzealous cloth sellers. They were begging, enticing and trying to force her to stop at their stalls and buy their goods.

'*Sister, na here de thing dey,*' said one rudely in pidgin English as he tried to pull her arm in the direction of his stall. She hadn't quite gotten over her anger with him when another waved at her face a feminine packet of cotton wool pads and said, '*My wife welcome. See wetin you talk make I keep for you.*'

She was a bit amused at this one. Some of them really sent you cracking. In the sole bid to sell their wares, they would virtually come out of their stalls to drag you out of your way. Many of them tried to speak with one as if they knew you for years.

She very much preferred the Eastern traders. They were warm and friendly. If you knew how to deal with them, you did not get cheated. They were very much known for their tactics of giving ridiculous prices. When you bargained, they would sometimes accept your offer of price, making you understand that it was on the grounds that you were the first customer or some lovely person. It would be later that you realised how much you lost in the deal.

The Hausas sold potatoes, cabbages and such foodstuffs, native clothes, slippers, beads, and foreign and local cassettes. They never tried to hawk their wares like the Ibos. They sat there. Their prices were fixed. If you couldn't pay their price, they left you alone. They could never be pressed further unless they so wished.

The Yorubas were known for their sour tongues. They lacked the Hausa and Igbo spirit. They insulted people who tried to bargain to their disfavour. They became malicious or moody when you purchased the same article from a neighbour trader.

The sons of the soil themselves, Tivs, were more of politicians, soldiers and the like. Those who were not, sold their own native foodstuffs or smoked away their pipes. They spoke their language to whoever called on them.

Martina was now walking out of the market. It was going towards 6 pm. Her hair was beautifully plaited and she was carrying a basket almost too heavy for her to carry comfortably. Before she could cross to the other side of the main road to where the buses were parked, various bus conductors and drivers rushed at her and tried to take the basket. They were all talking at the same time. She had difficulty trying to control them to leave her alone.

'Sister come. My motor don full. Jus now we go comot,' said one trying to have mastership over both her attention and her basket.

'Sister, enter my own now. Chance dey for front and good music dey flow,' another threw in.

Just as she was trying to make up her mind, she heard someone call out her name. It was Mr Edogbo, an Igalla man and tutor in her school. He too was coming out of the market with practically nothing other than a torchlight. He was opening the car boot indicating that he was going to help Martina home. When the bus drivers and conductors saw that they had lost a customer, they started their rude remarks.

'Look am. Because of only ten kobo, she wan go follow sugar daddy,' said one.

'Sister come enter. No mind. I fit borrow you ten kobo. Tomorrow you go give me,' another said.

When Martina got to the car, she soon realised Mr Edogbo had a companion with him who introduced himself as Ike. She turned down all their attempts to make her follow them for a quick go at some beer parlour under the excuse that she had a lot of cooking and work to do at home, and so she got them to drop her at her residence.

The next day was Sunday. Someone knocked the door. She didn't go to church but others in the house did, so the whole place was quiet. It was 9 am, and she was in bed day-dreaming. Instead of getting up to open the door, she called out weakly as to who the caller was, but the knocker maintained silence and persistently continued knocking until she was forced to get up and open the door. The face was strange. She couldn't place who the stranger was even though he was smiling so cheerfully. He was a fine man except that he had a lot of bumps on his face due to a recent razor shave.

At last, the stranger introduced himself as Ike Njoku and placed himself securely in her memory. Ike said he was travelling to Yandev and needed company and that he would be back latest by 4 pm. He didn't look a mean man. Moreover, he knew she would have to resume classes the following day. She wasn't trying to hatch out any dubious plans in her mind, but she found herself willing to go with him.

The drive to Yandev was beautiful. Ike was another clever and eloquent speaker. They ate well and drank beer at a very good restaurant. It was past two, and he entered one of the single rooms in the restaurant to rest. He invited her, but she refused and remained in the lounge. Ten minutes later, he came out to join her.

'Teeny, I feel very miserable without your company. I feel guilty that you are not enjoying the comfort of relaxing in an air-conditioned room. I would rather remain in the lodge while you could take a few minutes rest before we return to Makurdi.'

Ike seemed so decent and innocent. She never even gave it a second thought to doubt him. She did not feel strange and frightful at her openness towards this Ibo man she hardly knew a day back.

Eventually, she went to the room and collapsed on the bed. Ike came in five minutes later saying he was sleepy and that Martina was to wake him up when she had woken and wanted to be going back. This did not take place. Ike started talking. Martina was very much irritated. She was beginning to change her opinion about him after all. *So he didn't quite want to sleep.* Then she rose to prepare going. Ike was talking about marrying her. When Ike realised he had blundered, he apologised and tried another tactic. After all, she was a woman. If he tempted her with some sweet fruit like the apple of Eden, she was sure to fall.

'I am sorry I rushed my plans on you. It is love. Forgive me.'

Martina Vande was insistent. She wanted to go. Apart from Yakubu, she had received so many other minor bites. She had learnt her lesson. Men were selfish and they thought only of themselves.

'Maybe you are still too young,' Ike continued. 'I should wait for you. I will make sure Sammy Edogbo realises what you are to me so that he and your tutors will be lenient with you.'

She was quiet. She also heard him say he was not going to disturb her any further as he was too drunk to drive. She proceeded to lie down when she noticed he had faced the other direction. The room was cool and she felt a bit drowsy and tipsy. When she lay down, Ike turned and in a soft voice said he had only one question to ask her after which he knew he would be able to sleep. Martina was still quiet, so he drew closer and asked whether she even liked him at all. She got his breath and felt warm, so she shrugged her shoulders. After some seconds, she replied that Ike was on trial. In reply, he said he was so happy to hear her answer. He said he had not expected to hear that and for that, he was going to reward her with two dresses. But being a man, he would not know how to shop for a lady, and so he would give her sixty Naira to cover up for the two dresses.

Like an open flower to all suckers, she lacked the unique tact that only special flowers had for merciless suckers like the Venus fly trap did. She rather warmed up. She heard herself in her mind question her action, but she did not answer.

Ike sucked out a generous portion of nectar so that she suddenly felt remorse, guilty and empty. She sensed doom, but she did not try to bring her mind to register the fact. On the way to Makurdi Township, Ike was telling Martina to expect him the following day at 4 pm so that he would pick her up to do the shopping. Then he would have carried enough money for the shopping. All the same, he gave her ten Naira being all that he had on him.

Monday came, but Ike never did. By weekend of that Monday week, Martina did not need to console herself. She had been fooled again. Her spirit was brutally wounded. Her delicate framework was broken. Her soft petal heart crumpled up. It was only God that knew what amount of time could bloom her up again.

Ike had been a brute. She had never had it so rough before. Her memory was immediately renewed with incidents of suckers like Yakubu and others. She hated her private body. It wasn't hers anymore. She didn't know how to tear it off.

She also hated herself. She wished it was all a nightmare, but it wasn't.

At midnight, Martina Vande took pills to drug herself off to sleep. It was probably a winter sleep—hibernation. She would spring up in Heaven or Hell depending on Him.

Chapter 11
Tearful Passengers

Because everyone will do what is right, there will be peace
and security for ever... **Isaiah 32:17**

At number 6, Tarbong Avenue, there lived a merry woman.
Though she was a follower of Christ and knew so well that
God had issued a decree to refrain people 'putting asunder'
those beings He had joined together, she had gone against just
that and felt justified. She was already prepared with her case
on Judgement Day. Jesus, that very kind and understanding
man, was going to be her advocate. Her husband, Shaibu, was
a Mohammedan. She had a point there. It was also part of her
love for her God to win a soul through marriage with him.
Now see what happened. She was a good cook; a beautiful
woman; voluptuously busted and hipped. She was luxuriously
blessed with hair in all her hair facets. Everything about her
was promising. She was very enlightened about those
pleasurable things too. Alhaji was really lucky to have hooked
her type. What bait had he used? Only the angels knew. He
enjoyed everything about her and she too. She enjoyed his
wealth in particular. He was a good pupil too. He learnt fast
how to return pleasure for pleasure and not pleasure for
dissatisfaction.

Shaibu Ali was not too interested in all that Prophet Mohammed had preached. He could not even tell you what the five pillars of Islam were or the meaning of his name. Fridays did not find him in the mosque. Neither did the month of Ramadan find him fasting. He owned no Koran, praying mat or prayer beads. He knew Mohammed's Mecca at least. He was an Alhaji and a successful businessman.

Ali's household operated on the two faiths conveniently. They observed and celebrated the Moslem festivals as well as the Christian ones. That was how they brought up their kids— half-castes in religious faith. Ali was now in Ibadan and partially settled with an Alhaja. It was rumoured they lived a cat and dog life. If only Agnes, his Christian wife got to know, how happy she probably would have been, to think that Ali was alive and living elsewhere with another woman. Hadn't he promised that as an educated man, he would not behave like those Moslems who married a harem? Could he really be called a Moslem? That was the bait which he had hooked Agnes Effiong from Uyo in Cross Rivers State. Under the pretext of business, he had gotten himself another woman and settled her in Ibadan. Ali now had two homes: Lagos and Ibadan.

Their children had been donated to them by their Maker. They were all daughters of Eve. Perhaps that changed the wind of love to another direction. Then was it also not obviously visible that Ali looked like a son to Agnes, rather than a husband? She was too huge for him. Already his daughters were all looking like his sisters. They all took after their mother. They broke the standard number and time for eating. They ate between the three major meals, consoling themselves that they were taking snacks. As far as Ali was concerned, they were counted as meals. It seemed all his financial income was diverted to the kitchen pots. He couldn't be blamed for banking and saving elsewhere as he had done now but Agnes did. She was too jealous and hurt to forgive when the secret was spilled out about his 150 kilometres affair in Ibadan.

She had, during that marriage, tried to please him. Their children all bore Islamic names. Their first daughter, now eighteen, was Fatima by name. She was entitled to that name being the first daughter of her parents. The second girl who was twelve was Salamatu, though she was always being referred to as Sally. Then their youngest who was eleven was Habiba. She too, was known rather as Bibi a pet name kind of. They all now lived with their mother who was like a 'merry widow' at Calabar. They hadn't seen their father for almost two years now. They only knew he was in existence because he sent in fat cheques to their mother for their benefit. He sometimes wrote them endearingly. Sometimes, he remembered their birthdays.

Ali was fair. At forty-six, he was looking thirty due to his stature. He was also good looking no doubt. It was a fool who assumed that he had only Agnes and his Alhaja. He had a squint popularly known as "the four o'clock eyes". The left eye always pointed and looked elsewhere while the right eye sometimes aimed at you and so appeared in the opposite direction of the other eye. The poor eyes truly operated like the hour and minute hands of a clock. This Fatima, took from her father. She also took his small stature in comparison to her other two sisters and the striking face. She had neither surplus nor excess feminine endowments. When she wore a tee shirt tucked in trousers, she was very smart. She also took her mother's dark complexion and the gift of hair.

The other two girls were each different cases. They did not look like indigenes of their motherland. Maybe they got this streak from Ali. He almost did look foreign except that he had trademarks on his face that identified him immediately anywhere although some people were fooled. Salamatu and Habiba did not at all look their ages. Twelve-year-old Sally looked more like sixteen years. Her bust size was like two mountains of grapes. Her face was pimply with pimples. She was extremely fair, and in that was indeed the apple in her father's throat. She had been plump right from youth. One would have thought this fat girl would melt up all her fat as she grew up in to womanhood. Her pretty face and fair complexion attracted appreciative eyes. She was still her mummy's kid and in primary five. She was unlike her very intelligent sister who was already in her first year in university.

Habiba was another case. Indeed, it was as if God himself had given the couple three different cases for the whole world at large to judge. She blended both parents well. She was the prettiest of the three, though this was debatable. Though Habiba was only eleven, she was equally looking double her age. Luckily, she was not flabby like Sally. She was somewhat firm and stocky. She was also in primary five. Habiba had a lot of the Mohammedan tendencies. She loved her full Islamic name. She followed friends to the mosque and seized all the opportunities available to be identified with the rest of the Islamic world. When she was eight, she had asked her father to get her a Koran. That was shortly before the couple went into splinters. Habiba behaved like an adult. She could as well have been called the thorn in her mother's sole. She gave her mother pain and anxiety. The iron hand that Bibi lacked was surely not to be got from the mother.

Their mother, Agnes, gave her business an iron hand. She even added steel and metal to make it more successful. She no longer had time for men. She felt she was too fat to attract any interested man. Even if a man were blind in love to fall for her, she was ready to play the Good Samaritan and remove the obstacle from the blind eyes. Agnes Effiong was termed, "Madam". She also had all sorts of titles like Queen Mother, Big Mummy, Thick Madam, Holy Mary, Big Sister and so many others, but it was "Madam" that stuck out properly. She was known for her generosity when people paid a courtesy or financial call on her. She lived in comfort and style. Business was going on well; she had children and she was never in want. Even Ali was still being generous towards her. Maybe he felt guilty. After all, they were not divorced. He must have been feeling bad for the gnawing fact that he hadn't tried to see her or his daughters for almost twenty-four months. Even if business affairs were to take a three-quarter share of the blame, he would still be left with a quarter portion of the blame. He had no excuse. Anyway, he saw his Fatima from time to time. She served as his telegram mail to her mother. Only he wished Fatima was a son. She was very intelligent.

Ali had wanted sons as well. He felt the blow so much especially when it was an established fact that future childbirth would be a disaster to Agnes's health due to her fatness. However, Ali knew one thing was sure and basic: he missed her. She was a fantastic woman. There are certain things one feels like announcing to the world to correct its wrong notions and beliefs so as to make the ignorant world realise its conservative concepts as false facts. Fat women, the world held were no good, too sluggish and lazy at this or that; too heavy and slow for this or that. They were no better than condemned bad eggs. Ali was no longer in that school of thought. He would always be thankful to his stars who must surely have directed him to her.

She wasn't too fat when he had met her. She was about Fatima's size. With time, it increased especially a few years after Fatima's birth. To compare Agnes with Alhaja was to produce quite a strikingly different result. Alhaja was very much younger. She was in her late twenties and had recently given him his heart's desire: a son. Agnes was forty-two. She had just clocked forty when they went their different ways.

Still, in the opinion of Ali, the young blood of Alhaja could not beat the old one of Agnes. His young blood of a mistress disappointed him. He had always thought women in their thirties were only just arriving at the shore of passion, sexual peak and feminine warmth. In Alhaja's case, it was the other route. She was the "grab-grab" type and that was all. She was only a woman because her body was female. Her body was a mighty vault where a man could drown his own body. At twenty-nine, she was like sixty-nine. She must have begun life early and fast. Her heydays were over. All the fun and excitement had been exhausted. He was late. He should probably have met her when she was sixteen and thereabouts.

It was also his anxiety that Habiba would not become like Selimotu his Alhaja mistress. She only became an Alhaja the previous year while still in pregnancy, when she had followed him to Mecca. Otherwise, she was a nobody from her poverty-stricken home. However, he was consoled by his son.

Even now that he had got what he wanted, he was contemplating trying to stage a "go-back" to his beloved fat Agnes. But somehow, he felt it was impossible. Agnes could not afford to be counted amongst the harem, as she had always termed it.

Alhaja Selimotu loved money. Now she was getting it and enjoying it. Her parents were now living in a well-furnished flat. Many of her younger sisters, brothers and relatives were all properly placed on the ladder of life. School fees were promptly paid, scholarships obtained and her parents now shared a car driven by a chauffeur. She promised them soon another one so that they would each have one to themselves. One would have thought that a woman from such a background would have been humble and grateful and make a good housewife. Instead Alhaja was sharp, forward and brazened. One of her very poor relatives, too hopeless for any educational attainment whatsoever, was doing all the housework. The Alhaji was not even sure himself if he had ever tasted her own cooking. She was a Lagos woman. That was where he had met her in those days when he lived there permanently with Agnes and their daughters. Selimotu was very beautiful but only artificially. She was a hundred per cent when she was fully made up and well dressed. She reached down to twenty or lower if it wasn't the case.

Alhaji Ali Shaibu sometimes had time to himself. It was not always business. He was a big tycoon now and left all the running up and down to his 'errand boys' who would one day reach his present status and position. He was an importer of finished goods and did some distribution and contract jobs which all brought in huge profits. His mind went back to Selimotu. He was a fool not to have seen through her enticement. He regretted not heeding the fact those women of the ages around twenty-seven upwards were the frustrated desperate hawks. Anybody now mattered to most of them. All they wanted to was to be referred to as 'Mrs so and so' with certain number of kids, that's all. Then he remembered the case of Mr Feyisayo's wife, Yinka, who was about thirty-two, when he married her. Yet she was a good wife and a good example to argue against those who had negative thoughts about ladies who married late.

Ali did not derive any pleasure in their unions at night. Most times, she made excuses. When he insisted, she would then just behave like any gateman performing his duty by opening wide the gates. Those badly fallen and limp breasts, who or what had sucked them down? When you saw her dressed, you would think she had these proud young types that pointed crudely to the heavens. His mind examined the previous night's events. He had as usual had another very bad session. Where was all this leading him to? He never knew when he excited her. If he were to judge her on the basis of her usual and frequent dosing and falling asleep, then she was a very excited lover, and a very dull one at that. His torso, male and actions made no striking impact and impression on her. He was doing two people's jobs at the same time. Imagine that Selimotu behaving like a virgin, his having to direct her hands, her body and her almost everything. He hissed out like a very poisonous wounded snake.

It was afternoon during siesta time that he had ample time to ruminate these festered thoughts within him. Sleeping was impossible. He was not a happy man at peace. The maid, so to call her, had prepared a very poor meal. He was missing those Efik dishes and the other varieties. Bless Agnes for fond memories. It was through Agnes he had known what it was for a matured man to feel satisfied and blissfully happy in terms of pleasure. He learnt a lot. If he weren't lazy, he would put it all down to writing. Perhaps Selimotu needed to read up such things. He saw a woman's body like something comparable to a chess game. The key officials were there. You needed to know who played the part of the Queen, Bishop, Knights and so on. Likewise the same manner for a man's body. If one knew these officials, both partners put themselves automatically in to paradise.

He pictured Agnes: a real black beauty of her own kind, those big things up and down. Already, he was feeling excited and moved. Was she responding to his thoughts and feelings in telepathy? He never knew when he drifted into sleep.

Alhaja Selimotu was only Ali's mistress. They were not married in the real sense of the word. He still stayed at Lagos and occasionally visited Ibadan. With Selimotu, like a bad egg, he rarely visited. Even recently, she aborted his child and was taking pills to prevent pregnancy. *So she did not want to be his wife at all,* he thought. She had sacrificed her giving him a child in order to get all that she now had: land, houses, cars, fat bank accounts, gold and clothing. Alhaji knew. At least, he had a son, his heir, young Ali Baba-Isa Omolade Shaibu the second from Ogbomosho. He was always aware that despite the fact that Agnes and the girls consumed a lot of money in terms of food plus their educational and personal expenditures, he had spent more on only Selimotu and young Ali. He was sure he hated her. He was seeing through all her falseness. She was a frigid, hopeless parasite. He was surely going to continue on his self-development plans by channelling his beloved drifted canoe back to the shore.

It was now getting to three years since they had parted. Ali was missing Agnes, Sally and Habiba. He saw Fatima barely four months ago, but he was going to go down to Ibadan to see her again. It was going on to December. Fatima would go for the Christmas break to which she had been looking forward.

Fatima was an engineering student in her second year. She was in Queen Elizabeth Hall at the University of Ibadan. She was reading a letter from her beloved mother and wore a very serious face. She also had a second letter which she judged by the writing to be from Habiba. Her mother was informing her of the change of plans to come and pick her and that she had recently sacked the driver. She was pleading with the name of the dear Saviour to stay with Aunty Theresa at Ibadan. She was not to take public transport due to the increasing car accidents on the Nigerian roads. Her mother said she was fine. The two girls were already home for holidays. Habiba had done well but not Sally. They were also sad that they had lost the chance to come and see her at her hostel at Ibadan but were hopeful for a next time. Fatima was to come by air if she wanted to come home. If her money was not enough, she could go to her father or Aunt Theresa. She would be at the airport at Calabar with a car to take her home. She hoped she was doing well as usual. She ended by commending her to the keep of the merciful Lord of all.

Fatima's frown straightened and turned into an amused smile the contents of the letter still playing on her mind. She was thinking of that dear loving woman that was her mother. She surely loved her daughters. They were all that she had. It was because of them she existed. They were her life force and spur. This was going to be Fatima's third time in taking a

115

plane while at school. The first had been in her prelim year when she was going to the university for the first time. Her mother had come. She remembered how they both had cried when she was to return to Calabar. Then the second occasion had been when she was going for the long vacation in July. Now, this was going to be the third time. Her mother and driver had also come to pick her up for Easter. All other times, she had used public transportation which was not often. She normally stayed on the campus and she couldn't go home as often as she liked like those living within and around Ibadan. Now, her mind returned to one painful garage scene.

After her getting to the Uyo Garage, her mother did not go away immediately as expected. She had first of all noted the taxicab's number plate and with tears in her eyes, she had waited for the cab to be filled before leaving. When at last the taxicab started to move, she had lifted those mighty arms unmindful of the cramping pains and she had waved and waved while the tears did their own bit on her cheeks, chest and clothes. The pain of parting was stabbing but it didn't kill you. It could only break your strongest resistance. Fatima's resistance was broken down as she turned to look at her beloved mother for the last second before the cab disappeared out of view. Her mother had spat out mucus and with the same mouth, blew her darling daughter a sweet kiss.

She proceeded to open Habiba's letter. She got to her bedroom and even tried to settle down a little before reading it. She knew it was a reply to her own letter. The date showed the fact that it was before vacation. Sally and Habiba were now in form one at the Queen of Rosary, Calabar. The letter surprised her. It was a serious one. She wrote that their father had written to her to beg their mother for his forgiveness.

Also, he mentioned that he was relying on her to plead with their mother because she was very strong headed. If she, for example, could threaten their mother, she would be forced to succumb.

Fatima was surprised at her father's action. He hadn't even hinted a thing when she saw him only two weeks ago. He usually spent a few minutes chatting about her academic performances. He had dropped a fat pregnant letter for their mother and a letter each to her sisters along with some parcels which she knew contained trinkets like hers did. It therefore meant that their dad felt more relaxed with Habiba who was only now twelve. She wasn't jealous but just surprised, more so since he hadn't seen Habiba for almost three years now. She knew he communicated with them all through the medium of writing.

Her mind went back to her mother. How would she take or react to the news? She wondered what made her letter so bulky. She was sure it couldn't be money. Her father dealt with cheques not with raw cash. The envelope was so well sealed and so she did not want to open it. It was not that her mother would have done anything, but she loved to respect her still. Indeed, they were all like sisters to their own mother. She did not try to interfere with their private lives, but she made them realise that they were to have their way with men and get away with it and not the other way round.

Fatima remembered the occasion well when their mother had told them this. It was some six months after they had left their father. They were travelling by road from Uyo to Calabar where they had attended a divorce case in court. The proceedings went against the man. She spoke in their tongue since the driver was present. Immediately after the epistle, she kept quiet, and so did they. It seemed to dawn on them all of a sudden that though she had such a philosophy, she had not adhered to it since she was the one that backed away from their father. Fatima had sat in front with the driver while Bibi and Sally sat with their mother at the back. Fatima had turned backwards to tell Sally something she couldn't quite remember now. She had found Sally's eyes red and swollen with tears. Donna Summer's *Four Seasons of Love* was playing softly in the air-conditioned Mercedes car. It seemed to affect all their moods. Soon, Bibi had caught the contagious disease of weeping, and she wept softly. Their mother followed suit. Fatima did hers in front. Their mother played the chef role on them by serving them each some toilet tissue to clean out their noses and mop their eyes. Recounting all this, Fatima was sure that her mother would not welcome a reunion.

Agnes did not miss Ali much that is to say, if she did at all. She had in all those three years not replied any of his letters. She was not even happy to hear that he had a son. Someone had incurred his favour while she could not. Where she had failed and was defeated, another had succeeded. She felt all the more embittered. She was nevertheless happy to know that he still cared and longed for her company again. She was delighted too that he had not ignored the kids in terms of their financial welfare. The more she thought about this, the more she softened down. Then she made up her mind. She was not going to go back to Lagos. If he came down to her in Calabar, all would be well. He could also bring his little son who now was about a year and a half, but not the mother. This was what she decided when Habiba told her of their dad's letter written to her at school.

The Christmas was a happy one and well spent. Alhaji had sent the usual fat cheques and Xmas parcels. Only the cheques were much fatter this time. The whole family was aware of what was amidst. Their mother's fat letter told them all. Selimotu was not a wife even though she gave him a son anyway. She had dumped the little boy at Iseyin. She was a landlady, and Ali had no idea of where she now lived. Her tenants knew her by another identity and personality which did not fit into Ali's description in any way. He was just lucky to have known Selimotu's grandmother's place at Iseyin where he retrieved his young son from the reluctant frightened old woman who released the child under threats. She knew of Ali and her granddaughter's relationship. She too was not helpful in locating where Selimotu now lived. So she understood what the man was doing.

Ali wanted to come back to them with his little son. They should forgive him, and he was going to make it up to each of them to get their total pardon. Everything went according to plan. Shortly after the Xmas break but before the New Year, Agnes and the girls went to the Calabar Airport to receive him. He was welcomed with tears and kisses. He was very surprised to see the various changes in them. Even the young little boy, Lade and Ali were crying. The joy of seeing them all was too much for him even as a man to control. All the way back to number 6, Tarbong Avenue, the passengers of the Saloon 504 Peugeot car sniffed on and on. Shoulders jerked and chests heaved violently. Fatima had now cooled down a bit. She was thinking of a similar incidence to this one. Three years aback. She was comparing events. To her everything was basically the same except for a few obvious differences. Then, they were leaving their father, but now, he was the one coming to them. The tearful passengers then were her mother, her two sisters and herself, but now, her father and his little son, their brother were among them. They had wept silently and briefly, but now they all wept uncontrollably and for the first five minutes of the trip.

Fatima could not believe the amount of water she saw come out from her mother's eyes. Probably, her mother's fat comprised water all through and through. Their father suddenly became a man. He was saying that they were not to spoil the reunion by being "tearful passengers".

Chapter 12
Love for Sale

He will fulfil the desires of those who fear Him…
Psalm145:19

From the back of the house, sitting on a chair that backed the wall, the world looked so beautiful. The time was 5 pm. The sky and the cloud had blended together to produce a bleached blue sky. The breeze blew making all the leaves, branches of trees and flowers to dance. The world was really beautiful and Ugo felt that way. What was not beautiful was the unsolved and unsolvable problems man had and which he had caused on himself.

Ugo's peaceful and solitary mood was ended abruptly when he heard Chuks whistling.

'Sailor Boy, I am here.' He got up and stretched himself a bit. 'Come and join me here.'

Chuks had earned himself that name while they were all at the University of Nsuka. The way he scored high grades in all his courses made it appear as if he always sailed through all obstacles without any difficulty. They were both from Owerri in Imo State. Though Chuks was married, he still retained a good relationship with his bachelor friend who was older. Ugo got another chair and placed it beside his, and the two friends got talking.

'Ugo, why do you sit idly like an old man?'

'I am an old man,' he answered wryly.

'I see, so why are you not snuffing your nose or going about with a stick poking your nose about like old men do?' Chuks asked laughing.

'Sailor Boy, stop worrying Gold Fingers. Don't you see I am on a serious level this evening?'

'Gold Fingers!!! If you are serious while as a bachelor, what will happen when you are married?'

'Till then. So married people are the only sensible people to be described as serious? Heh! *Ugochukwu Obiechina!* Where is your wife so that you can be referred to as a serious person?' he ended stiffly and unsmiling.

'Ugo, where is all your humour? You are easily irritated. What is wrong old chum?' Chuks inquired studying his friend closely and realising the moody state of his friend.

'Chuks, you have not even observed that Ngozi and I have not been going out together of late. Yet you say nothing and pretend.'

'Oh!' answered back a shocked Chuks.

Chuks kept quiet and looked pensive for several seconds. Who would believe that Ugochukwu the darling of girls and women at school was still single? His parents were middleclass working people. He himself read *Quantity Surveying*. He was a ladies' man, tall, broad-chested, and not too dark with muscled tight skin. Indeed, everything he seemed to touch brought him good luck, hence his nickname "Gold Fingers". But somehow, when he touched women, his good luck ran out. At school, he had exchanged women with regular ease. He was not serious then. He assumed his good looks and promising future would get him his heart's desire when finally he was ready to quit bachelorhood. At last, Chuks broke the silence.

'What is wrong with Ngozi, again? Ugo, you have to realise that there is no angel on earth. Maybe you expect too much from women and…'

'Expect too much what?' Ugo rudely cut in. 'Are you advising me to go in for anybody? Why didn't you marry that Bendelite girl? Have you forgotten that you lost interest in her simply because of her inability to socialise, and what was the other?' he asked in a quarrel kind of tone.

'Too petite for me,' Chuks completed. 'Ugo, look, don't get me wrong. I was not even trying to advise you. I was just giving you some philosophy.'

'Chuks, let's go in. These sand-flies will finish us here.'

The two friends went in. Chukwuka Odi, called Chuks for short, was not as tall as Ugo. Somehow, he had ended up in business which was not doing badly for him. Shortly after his wedding, he and his wife started having financial problems. Chuks had spent so much to have his wife as is customary for Ibos. They hardly had anything to eat. Also, he was in huge debt.

Gone was the sweet side of the affair, and bitterness set in. His government work was hardly able to see them through. He begun by selling iron rods until by luck, he got a supply contract with the Mobil firm. His wife, Chinyere, who was an NCE teacher, was not particularly beautiful, but they got on well together because they seemed to fit each other. She too had a business-like spirit because she started a small poultry business to supplement their income during the rainy days.

Now, her poultry business was the talk of the town. From his own experience, Chuks realised that women changed subtly after they were married either for the better or worse. Still, everything depended very much to a large extent on the man. This was what Chuks had earlier on during their conversation wanted to point out to Ugo, but he was misconstrued.

When the two friends got into the house, they resumed their conversation.

'Look, Chuks, Ngozi and I are great friends. I don't have any problem as regard bride price, but somehow, this girl is evasive.'

'Meaning?' asked Chuks who was not quite in the light.

'That she doesn't want marriage between us. That's all. Why should I continue wasting my time and money for a girl who is not interested?'

'I think I know Ngozi's problem,' Chuks said as if to produce a solution to the issue. 'All these graduate corpers look above themselves. Maybe Ngozi is looking for a very wealthy man and all that.'

Ugo did not want to say what was uppermost in his thoughts. Since his friend had married an NCE, he was bound to feel negative towards women who were degree holders, but he did not say this. No Chuks, you are wrong. Actually, Ngozi feels she is still too young to marry. You know she is only twenty.'

'Twenty? How manage? She must have entered Uniport at 16!'

'Yes. Something like that. So that is really her problem.'

'Okay. You say you are good friends? Then keep the relationship going till she is ready. What are you talking again?' beamed Chuks excitedly.

'Sailor Boy, you are sailing in the wrong direction. I want to marry soon, this year possibly.'

'I see. So?'

'How can I go on with a girl who can't make up her mind? For how long shall I wait?'

'No problem. Convince her. Make up her mind for her. You said the love is there.'

'Easier said than done.'

'Well, listen to my last advice,' Chuks said as he rose looking at his watch. 'Why not stop smoking and drinking till you are seriously involved.' Then he laughed his rich laughter as he made towards the door, 'It's getting to 5 o'clock chum. I must be going.'

'Where are you running to? It's too early. I haven't even served you anything. I know my apartment is bare. Chuks, wait and have something now.'

Chuks merely shook his head negatively and laughed.

'Well, thank you for your advice. Not bad really, but if I took it, my new wife will find me a stranger when we get married, and there the trouble starts, you see.' For the first time that evening, he relaxed and laughed richly along with his friend who was by now out of the house.

'Okay,' said Chuks with a wave, 'cut off the habit completely and forever.'

Ugo laughed and waved back. He did not escort his friend because he wanted to go and see a few friends or so before retiring for the night.

As he watched his friend walking smartly down the Elekahia Road, he envied him. At 37 with three kids, his figure was trim. He was well disciplined. He didn't indulge in unnecessary pleasures. Rather than using his car all the time, he sometimes made his appointments on foot. He had walked all the way from Trans Amadi Road to Elekahia Road. He neither smoked nor drank beer and other such liquors except on certain rare occasions. He had a wife and did not have a bulging stomach. He had eaten several times at Chuks' house. Chinyere was not a bad cook, at least judging from his own standard. Yet, he who was supposed to be fit and trim had a slight bulge of the tummy. As he walked back home, he gave it a serious thought to resolve to refrain from smoking and drinking.

Ngozi Okoli who read French at University of Port Harcourt, [Uniport] was doing her NYSC [National Youth Service Corps] at one of the state secondary schools in Port Harcourt. She had met Ugochukwu at a housewarming party organised by Mr Okeke who was Ugo's friend at the P&T [Post and Telecommunication]. Their relationship had been on for some five months. She had got to realise his sincerity in wanting marriage between them. She felt scared. *So soon. Imagine her, a small rat, getting married! What did she know?* In fact, when she had discussed it with some close friends, they had almost laughed off their heads. One of them, Ibinabo, had said she couldn't imagine Ngo with a swollen belly and a serious disposition on her face, supervising the preparation of a meal in the kitchen!!! Ngozi had nothing against Ugo. She was not too young to fall in love because she had had friends and affairs at school, but Mrs Obiechina...No! Three or four years' time, maybe yes.

This had been the problem of Ugo while at school. He had not been serious too. He had reasoned like Ngozi. He had felt that life was not to be rushed but to be enjoyed while the opportunities were there. During his NYSC at Ikare in Ondo

State, he had decided to become serious because he realised it was not a bad idea at all. Then he was about twenty-eight. He was one of those victims who schooled late because of the Biafran war. As he was buttoning his shirt in the bedroom, he recalled one pleasurable incident with one Nike Adelagun.

He had reached the house where he lived as a corper in the Boy's Quarters in the Staff Quarters. He was surprised to see his door open and he was apprehensive. Only few good friends of his knew he kept the key on top of the tanker at the back of the kitchen. What was more, somebody was cooking something delicious in the kitchen because the aroma from the kitchen told him so. To his greatest surprise and joy, he saw Nike, who was serving at Ondo. They had been in the same squad during the orientation programme and they had noted their posting addresses when it was released. That day Ugo saw Nike, he was so overwhelmed with joy that he was speechless for a few seconds. At last, he regained his composure and greeted her in the Igbo language.

'Nike!!! *Nno Kedu?*'

She had in turn shocked him by answering him back in correct Igbo. It had been four months after their orientation service and they had each exchanged letters thrice.

'So my dear, how did you find this place out and who opened the door for you?'

'Easy. I asked questions, that's all. Also, I am familiar with Ikare. You know I am from Ondo State. As for your door key, I saw something like a scorpion on top of your tanker when I was surveying the general view of things. *Sha* it turned out to be your key which I tried with 100% luck.'

'God, I have to find a new venue for it. Oh, maybe you came to see dad and mum and not us,' he kind of accused.

'*Ah noo oh! Sebi* my parents live at Akure. Don't make silly remarks. Come inside now and see what I have done. I have been here since 11 am. I arrived from Ondo yesterday and put up with Funke Adejobi. You know her?'

'No I don't.' He hardly listened to her because he was so struck and overcome with surprise at what he saw. Because as they conversed later, he realised he knew Funke very well. She had been in their squad but had rearranged for her reposting to her own state immediately after the orientation.

Nike had given the house a new outlook. Everywhere was neat and tidy. She had also prepared fried rice and vegetable salad, making use of whatever ingredients she had found in the fridge and garden. He had nothing against Nike. He never for one day thought it wise to propose to her. He had assumed there would be a downright rejection from her because of their ethnic differences. If only he had known. He had just enjoyed a causal relationship with her and let her slip by. He felt very bitter because she was later married to another fellow Ibo.

Immediately after his service, he was about twenty-nine. He still had his good looks, nice sideburns and a moustache. Even Nike had commented on his romantic eyes. Was it Stella or Rachel Davies who had made a remark on his flashy smiles in his third year at the university? With his dressing, he was very particular just like a woman. He only used medicated soaps, moisturising creams, talc powders and strongly scented perfumes. His complexion was really attractive in itself. Then he even had the appearance of a well-to-do manager of a bank that worked in an air-conditioned office and lived in an air-conditioned house. His skin was remarkably clear and smooth except for the fine manly hairs he had on his chest, arms and legs.

As he had just finished his NYSC then, he was considered too poor to be able to meet up with the demands of marriage rites imposed on him by his people. He would need not less than N5,000 for the traditional aspect alone. So his bachelorhood had extended on for five years more. Then he was ready but the women were not ready for him or his "Gold Fingers" now brought him bad luck. The case of his affair with Ijeoma was very pathetic. He even sponsored her NCE programme. All was going well. He had spent not less than N7,000 throughout the course of his relationship with Ijeoma and on her family. Then his good luck ran out. Ijeoma was not prepared to drop her Cherubim and Seraphim religion for his Catholic one. Both families had no agreement on this either and that was the end. He was again left bankrupt for some time.

Now a matured man of thirty-eight, he was still single. His mother in particular was putting pressure on him. Going home to the village these days was not worth it. Why was he so unlucky? It was out of sheer frustration and loneliness that he took to the habit of smoking and drinking. All his age grade mates, old school friends were all married with kids, and he was yet to find a wife. At the rate at which he was going, his age would soon become a disqualifying factor. He remembered what Deborah had said. She was a one-time girlfriend after Ijeoma. She was a bit too much on the plump side, and he wondered what kind of picture they would cut after three years of marriage. Deborah had said men never looked their ages. So her own way of reckoning their ages was to look into their nostrils and on their heads. A few strands of white or grey hair told enough and she would be off on her heels. Apart from Deborah's excessive weight, she was very untidy and careless. There were two occasions when she had lost money. The first time was N25 while the second one was N40. Deborah had not shown enough remorse. That had ended his interest in her.

Here in Lanre's house, he was drinking a bottle of cold Berger Duff beer. To be with Lanre was to be kept laughing continually all the time. He was a great jester and very humorous. He too was a bachelor but younger. He was thirty-five years. He had a good job with the International Merchant Bank, a posh car and a well-furnished flat. Whereas, Ugo was thirty-seven after he recovered from the Ijeoma episode. Then he was able to purchase a second-hand Beetle to make his bait on women stronger.

Girls were seen all round the clock in Lanre's house. It was even rumoured that he had slept with six of them at a go. When he was asked to verify the allegation by close friends, he even added one to the number and laughed it off.

'Cold Fingers, have you heard?' Unlike everybody else who called Ugo "Gold Fingers", Lanre called him, "Cold Fingers" because according to him, it was the coldness of his hands that drove his women away.

'Yes, heard what?' asked Ugo in an excited voice but with only one of his ears on the ground, since he could not expect anything serious from this joker of a friend.

'I'll be dropping my bachelorhood this year.'

'What!' exclaimed a shocked Ugo. 'No man. I don't believe you. You of all people? When did you start and who is this unlucky girl?'

Lanre greeted all his questions with an infectious laughter which infected Ugo, and they both laughed heartily. Ugo sipped the last drains of his beer and watched his friend to see what explanation he had to offer. Sometimes, the clown of a man spoke sense.

'And so my dear Cold Fingers, I am also pleased to inform you that you too would be promoted to husband-hood this year.' With that said, they both laughed again.

'Lanre, when will you grow up and you want to get married? You are not serious. I have to show you the way,' Ugo said heartily.

'Cold Fingers, listen; stop talking rubbish and making noise!'

The way he said this made Ugo laugh afresh again until both men were laughing. After some time of soberness, Lanre started off again. 'Cold fingers, if Mohammed will not go to the mountain, the mountain will go to Mohammed. That is my version, and I have complied with it. Ask me how, my brother?' He asked this with a twist of his long neck. He was a very dark, lanky, hairy man. He looked twenty-seven, and sometimes his unserious attitude towards his life made him appear younger.

Ugo did not ask how in compliance with his question but started to laugh again.

'Pocket your laughter first,' Lanre exclaimed looking a bit serious. Pulling a letter from one green file on the table, he gave Ugo to read. What Ugo read made his eyes open very wide. The date was recent. Lanre was indeed serious. The letter read:

Dear Lanre,

I read your advertisement on "Husband for free sale". I fit your desired requirements. I am really fascinated at your photograph which turned out well in the Weekend Newspaper.

I hope we shall make it together with God on our side. I have attached my own photograph and residential address as you requested.

I expect a visit from you in the near future.

Yours to be

Chizoba Chikwelu

No 411/SA, Johnson Crescent

Upper Nile, Enugu.

The photograph attached revealed a youthful cheerful lady of about twenty-two or thereabouts. Ugo was dumbfounded. He read the letter three times.

'Lanre! From Port Harcourt to Enugu, how are you going to achieve this?'

Lanre laughed a bit and in a serious tone replied, 'The relationship has already been struck. The next thing now is wedding. Ugochukwu, I will strongly advise you follow my footsteps. If you dote on the saying that says, "too many fishes in the ocean", you will discover that the fishes are many and sweet but too many bones.'

This time neither of them laughed. Each was wrapped in serious contemplation. Ugo nodded his head positively. He didn't find it a bad idea.

Chapter 13
The Temptation

Choose my instruction rather than silver… **Proverbs 8:10**

In the early morning as the day is breaking, it is not sure of which weather to break for the day. It was therefore neither raining nor sunny. The weather combined some drizzles of rain and some kisses of the sun's rays.

Sometimes, many people are made victims of this type of weather because they are unduly exposed to idleness, daydreams, fantasies, and wishes. Odula, an Idoma girl, like every normal human being, had been awoken by the crowing of the pastor's cock which was the biggest in the village and reputed for its loud, clear ringing crow in the early hours of dawn. She then proceeded to do the normal duties and routine of the morning. She plunged into her mouth a rather fat and bulky chewing stick, and then she washed her face and tied a miserable-looking wrapper over her young innocent body. She was indeed a young girl. It was quite easy to reckon her age. Her grandfather and his family had moved into that village of Udu-aka seven years ago. Her little brother had been a toddler with mucus running down his little nose bridge.

She remembered the occasion very well. She had however been too young to understand why her grandfather, her mother, Ojomo, and her baby brother had left their beloved village of Umah and without their father. There had been no undue quarrel between her parents then. Her mother had been rather happy then, she had thought, likewise her father. He looked quite content with life. Oh, but then, that was her childish thought seven years back. Odula was now a matured girl of fourteen. In the past, her mother, Ojomo had consoled herself and Oko that their father had decided to go to the big city of Oturupo to acquire more wealth. On his return, he would bring plenty of nice things for the children.

When she was about ten, her mother had got tired of this same old tale every day and decided to tell Odula about the whole matter. Ojomo had been married happily to Ube, and after two years, their first baby child was born—Odula. It had not been easy conceiving a child and neither was childbirth. After patiently waiting for six years, little Oko came to the scene, but his coming brought problems. Apart from his being delivered by the legs, his mouth was full of teeth! This was considered to be an ominous sign to the people of Umah Village. A famous dibia who looked into the matter announced to the villagers his findings:

'This woman has a disease. It is a very uncommon one but dangerous because other women may get it. Neither mother nor child is to be harmed, but she must strictly keep indoors for seven years.'

It was such a blow for the woman who became even more devoted to her husband. Alas. Such is the nature of men. Shortly after this incidence of Oko's birth, rumours were heard that Ube was courting some young girl elsewhere in the village. Ojomo confirmed this, and she decided to stealthily pack her belongings and that of her children and go to her grandfather because she had no parents. When Ojomo and the kids finally arrived at her grandfather's house, he had felt pity for his granddaughter.

'My dear child, this place is too near to your husband's house. You need to go somewhere else where rumour of your misfortune has not done havoc. Your own father's village will be the best place.'

Oko, now six years old, was failing in health. Upon consultation of a dibia, it was known that his ailment was due to the fact that his spirit was a twin to his father's and therefore the child had to be taken to his father's home at Umah. A half day's journey from Udu-aka village by foot.

Odula was now alone. Her not-too-old though able grandfather had accompanied her mother and brother. She was still busy with her morning chores of the day which had far advanced for it was now about 8 o'clock. After she had washed herself, tidied the little humble hut of a house and had even paid a homage call to their little farm, she then settled herself on a large stone and was shifting cassava. It was then her mind wandered off on various issues… All of a sudden like lightening appearing on a sunny but windy day, her mind became conscious as it reflected over a mischievous thought.

Odula had slowly been responding to the advances of Emi, the village pastor's son. Emi was three years older. When Odula was about nine, he had always admired her keenly, though it was then on an innocent basis. The pastor had sent his son for schooling at the city, and Emi was seen only during the major festivals while all his other holidays were spent with a childless aunt of his. Indeed, Mr Pawa, the pastor, was known to possess the greatest number of children in the village. He had seven daughters and five sons. Emi was the first. Emi, now tall and fair like his mother with thick lips like his maternal grandfather, was now a very attractive and handsome youth of seventeen.

Once at the stream, when Odula broke her water pot, he had confessed to her that he loved her and that she was the most beautiful girl he had ever known and seen. Before this, he had been making meaningful passes and signs to Odula to make her realise his interest in her. He had even asked her when would be the best time to see her privately and alone, in a secluded area. Whenever she had the right answer, she was to lurk around his father's house and whistle four times.

Now, thought Odula to herself, *this time is a good opportunity…*

Chapter 14
Exchange Is no Robbery

Don't hope to gain anything by robbery… **Psalm 62:10**

A thriller movie was going on at the Oduduwa Hall, at the University of Ife. The hall was silent. A scene of tension was going on in motion. Teju sneezed, and someone else whistled rudely as a compliment.

'Oh, bless you,' a soft male voice greeted her from behind.

'Thanks,' she replied without even looking back. Teju nudged at her partner beside her and whispered an accusation.

'Bush boy. You couldn't even greet me when I sneezed,' she accused in a playful tone.

'Oh, did you! When? You know I must have been very engrossed in the film,' whispered Olumide.

Teju did not say anything. If she did, a little quarrel might ensue. Petty issues flared up the fiery temper of Olumide so easily. They had been getting on along for about a session. Sometimes, they got on very well, and at other times, Teju was sure she disliked him. One thing about Olumide was that he always expected the best out of others. He did not care whether he too gave the best of himself. Only last week, Olumide had scolded Teju in front of her roommates. How many times had she pleaded with him to stop that habit? Yet, when she had told him, he took offence and kept to himself for two days. By the third day, Olumide apologised to Teju and he bought her some suya. That was one thing she liked about Olumide. When he was in the wrong, he apologised.

After the film, Olumide was walking Teju to her hall of residence. All the time Teju was chatting about the film, Olumide was a bit too silent. Then he broke the silence.

'So Teju, who is the guy that greeted you in the hall?'

'Which guy is that?'

'Do not pretend; the guy who greeted you when you sneezed.'

'Oh, I remember. I don't know him.'

'Then why did you answer him.'

'Ah, Olumide, you have come again. I thought you said you did not know when I sneezed. I think you are a dangerous person.'

'You mean you don't know Tunji? We are both in Fajuyi Hall. He is not in our class. He is a year ahead of us.'

'So? Why should you think I ought to know him?'

'Because you both danced together at that party. Remember now?'

'You are being funny. Am I expected to remember all the guys I dance with? If you want to annoy me this night, let me go. Good night.'

Olumide did not answer. It was just like him to get angry over petty things that didn't matter.

Unlike both Teju Akinola and Olumide Fadipe who were third-year students in the Faculty of Sciences, Tunji Fayemi was a fourth-year student in the Faculty of Medicine. He had taken a keen interest in Teju since he first met her during a dance at a party. He could not forget her. She was slim, moderately built with a full bosom and very broad hips. She had danced very gracefully with him. Tunji liked beautiful women, and Teju was no exception. He did not think himself very handsome, but at least, he had gentle manners which most women adored in men.

After the film, he had walked towards the direction of Teju's hall. He made sure that neither of them saw him. He had thought he would have been able to get a chat with Teju. Judging from the way Tunji saw Teju and Olumide sit in the hall, he felt their relationship was not very deep. One could judge the relationship between two partners at the Oduduwa Hall from how they sat, conversed and behaved. Left to Tunji, Teju and Olumide behaved formal, and he felt he had a chance to try his luck. What was more, they hardly lingered at the "Lovers Park". The "Lovers Park" was the name given to the Mozambique Hall Car Park. Tunji lingered around the female hostel for some minutes. He had watched Teju go into Block M. He wondered why all of a sudden he felt the urgent urge to see and speak to her. He considered going into the hall to seek her room out, but he decided against it and trekked his way back to Fajuyi Hall. There were other ways he thought. And time too. It was still the month of February.

For three days following the incident of the night Olumide took Teju to watch a film, Olumide did not call to see her. During lectures too, he avoided her. A cold war ensued. Olumide felt that Teju had behaved saucily and had no right to have spoken down to him the way she did that night. He knew he had asked her silly questions concerning Tunji, but still, it was out of his protection and love he felt he had for her. So he felt that she ought to break the ice between them first this time.

Teju on her own part felt that she was allowing Olumide to ride on her head by being too over possessive. She felt insulted by the implications of what his silly questions meant to her. She too felt that he owed her an apology. Though in her hearts of hearts, she felt that it had been a bit bad of her to have bid him a good night the way she did and walked off.

On the fourth day however, during a lecture, Teju scribbled some words down on a note and folded it. The note was passed from hand to hand to reach Olumide at where he sat at the other side of the room. In the note, she wrote that she was very surprised that he could keep malice over such a little affair with her. That however, she didn't like their present situation and was sorry he didn't see with her that night. Olumide too passed a note back to her that gave a message of his wanting to see her after the lectures and under the almond tree at the back of the auditorium in which they were in.

After the lecture they met.

'You stubborn girl.'

'I am not stubborn. It is you who is trying to be stubborn.'

'How?'

'I don't know for you.'

'What do you mean by that?'

'Well, it was you who brought up the Tunji issue.'

'So you still remember his name. And what is wrong with bringing up the issue? All I expected was a simple answer from you and not for you to be tossing with my questions.'

'Yes, Sir. I see,' Teju said to sound funny.

The way things were going, Olumide was ready to start another quarrel. They both laughed to Teju's remark and walked towards the Students Union Building [SUB]. They resumed their conversation as they walked towards the SUB.

'Teju, I will be travelling this weekend to Lagos. I want to see what I can collect from my old man.'

'Don't tell me you are broke again, Olu?'

'Look at you. What are you saying? My pocket money has to run out sometime, you know.'

'I know. I only wish you had given me some other excuse for going home rather than that you are broke. It makes me feel guilty.'

'Why? Don't be funny. You are making it sound as if I want to blame you.'

'Ah, where did you get that idea from?'

'That is what you imply about being guilty and all that. I really don't like the way you talk at times,' Olumide said hotly.

'What is it I have said again? You just like getting angry over nothing.'

'I see. Well, I am going for lunch at the buka. You care to come?'

'No. I really don't feel hungry. Thanks.'

'Indeed. I know you are now beginning to feel you must not make me more broke, isn't it?'

For a reply, Teju hissed and said, 'Olumide, where will these your costly jokes get us to?' With that said, she went away.

That same Thursday evening, Olumide called on Teju. He told her he was sorry he upset her, but he realised that his apology could not lift the damp mood off Teju. He tried to be intimate, but she would not budge. At last, he announced that he was going.

'Well, Teju dear, I can see you are not feeling well. You have rejected all of my offers in making this evening groovy for us. See yah.'

'See yah and safe journey. When do I see you next?'

'Do you really care?'

'You again.'

At this, Olumide went to her bedside and in the vernacular petted her with some endearing words and kissed her. She returned the kiss. They bade each other a good night and Olumide left.

On Saturday morning, when Teju was taking her bath, she tried to identify the owner of the voice that had greeted her at Oduduwa Hall. *A Tunji… A year four student… Had danced with me…* Try as hard as she could, she could not place this Tunji.

Saturday afternoon at 3 pm, someone knocked on Tunji's room door. It was Shade, his roommate's girlfriend. She had probably come to spend the siesta or something else with Lana, his roommate. The usual greetings and sweet talk were exchanged between them. Lana's voice brought him back to reality.

'Oh boy, have you got your letter? I saw it on the desk at the Porter's Lodge. I hadn't known I would be coming this way. It is still there.'

'That's good news, Paddy.'

'I thought so too. The writing looked feminine.'

Tunji laughed himself out of the room. He had got the message. Lana wanted to be alone with Shade.

Tunji envied Lana. His affair with Shade reminded him of Jumoke, his ex-girlfriend. They had got on fine and had suited themselves perfectly fine. Somehow Jumoke had been biased or had got the impression from nooks and corners that he was a playboy and was taking her for a ride. Unfortunately for him, he seemed to have unconsciously given that impression of himself. In his attempt to please Jumoke, he had been a very friendly guy. Too friendly. He was all full of smiles and cheers when he came across Jumoke's friends. To impress her further, he even visited a few of them. And that must have been how the rumour had started.

'Hi, Jumy, we saw Tunji in our room today.'

'Really?'

'Ah, yes. I am sure he had come to see one of my roommates. But when he saw me, he pretended as if it had been me he had come to see.'

'And you know, that is not the first time. He happens to frequent Kike's room in the pretext of calling to say hi. But when she is not there, he still stays on,' another girl will chirp.

'To see who? Please tell me,' Jumoke would plead.

'Eh, these medical boys, you can't say for them o!'

That was how Jumoke left him, all because of wild rumours without a basis. Most medical students always had that problem. It was easier befriending girls from other campuses.

Just in case Lana was serious, he checked the table at the Porter's Lodge. No letter. He decided to go to the Post Graduate Hall [PG]. He could watch the draught players at their game. It was much fun watching those matured guys at their game rather than the hot-headed youths of Fajuyi Hall whose attentions were always diverted whenever they saw a lady pass. Just as Tunji was getting to the PG Hall, he changed his mind. He decided to make a U-turn and head for the SUB. There was a Maxi Supermarket on the ground floor. He would glimpse at a few newspapers and magazines sold in front of the Maxi Supermarket and return to the room. Lana and Shade would have finished with themselves for whatever purpose they had wanted the room to themselves.

Tunji entered the Maxi Supermarket. He had nothing in particular to buy. Many students did that as routine when they were at the SUB. When he got to the section where cosmetics were sold, who did he see? Teju. But she did not recognise him. When she looked up at him briefly to see whether it was a familiar face, she saw a stranger's face that was smiling knowingly at her.

'Hi. I hope you are better now. You had symptoms of cold last week. Can you remember that someone greeted you when you sneezed?'

'Okay! Yes I do remember. So it was you? I was beginning to wonder what you were talking about initially. Okay. I am much better now. Thanks.'

'Tunji Fayemi is my name, and yours?'

'Teju.'

'Oh, that is a sweet name. I have a cousin who is very beautiful like you with that name too.'

'I beg your pardon; you can say that again, flatterer.'

'No, I am not flattering you.'

Just then Teju sneezed again.

'Oh, bless you. Why not try this remedy. Take two tablets of Septrin and rub your chest with Mentholatum. You will be okay for good.'

Teju laughed. 'You sound like a doctor.'

'I hope to become one anyway.'

'Okay, yes. Someone mentioned it to me.'

'Someone? Who?' Tunji asked, taken a back a bit.

'Okay, it was my boyfriend. He said he knew you.'

'When did he say this?'

'Oh, it was that same night you greeted me when I sneezed. He was able to identify your voice.'

Tunji felt Teju was lying, but he didn't say so. Somehow, Olumide had guessed Tunji's intentions. They were not really friends or even acquaintances, but as members of the same hall, they met once in a while. They had met each other on Friday. Each of them had tried to avoid the other.

Tunji and Teju strolled out of the Maxi.

'Where are you going now?' Tunji asked.

'Nowhere in particular.'

'You know what I have noticed?'

'What?'

'Both our names begin with a T.' Then he laughed at this.

'Oh! What an observation.' She too re-joined in the laughter.

After a few seconds of silence, Tunji continued. They had climbed upstairs of the SUB and had settled themselves on a seat.

'Teju, I have known you before today, you know.'

'Is that so?' Teju feigned ignorance.

'Yes. Do you remember one get together that was held at the Fajuyi Common Room sometime in January?'

'Okay. Yes, I was there. Were you there too?'

'Of course, yes. We even danced together.'

'Did we?'

145

Somehow, Teju found herself wanting to chat on and on with Tunji. He was quiet-spoken by nature. They conversed on a wide range of topics at the SUB parlour where they sold drinks and snacks. He was very interesting to be with. He had a romantic way of looking at Teju when she talked. Teju did not have to fear whether any of her statements might be misinterpreted. She did not feel guilty for having accepted to go with Tunji to watch a movie at Oduduwa Hall that evening.

The film turned out to be purely comic. It was a very funny one. At least, Teju found it that way. To her surprise, Tunji was calm.

'Aren't you enjoying the film?' Teju had asked.

'Well, it is not bad, but it is not my type.'

'Which is your type?'

'Horror, thriller, espionage and the likes.'

'Hmm. You must be a tough person.'

'I am not necessarily so, but with time, I am sure you will find the real truth.'

'About?'

'Me.'

All Teju could do was to shake her head with a smile on her face.

After the film, he walked her down to her hostel. He thanked her for keeping the evening with him and hoped that they would have more of such evenings together. They bade each other good night and Tunji walked back to his room. He felt light at heart and happy. He could hardly wait to get back to his room and daydream about Teju. He would visualise how close he really wanted them to be in reality. To him, this was a healthy habit. Dreams really could come true.

On Sunday evening, Olumide called on Teju at about 8 pm. She was alone.

'Olu dear, are you back?'

'Thanks, darling. I am back.'

'What did you bring back for us?' Teju teased.

'The whole of myself in one piece.'

'That's the greatest gift, but are you sure some people did not steal some part of you?' Teju asked jokingly.

'I should ask you that,' Olumide put in.

'*En-en*, I asked you first.'

'Okay. Sincerely, no, and take me for my words.'

'I trust you, darling, and you know I was only joking.'

'So how was your weekend?' Olumide asked.

'Eh, what is a weekend without you, my dear? I have missed your company, warmth and love.'

'No, Teju. Don't tell me all that. Bolaji said he saw you at the movies.' Bolaji was a fellow classmate in the same faculty and department with Olumide and Teju.

'Ah, my darling, I am still coming to that, don't rush me.' Teju proceeded to tell Olumide how she had come about meeting Tunji and how he invited her to the movies. She also made it clear that Tunji's intentions towards her were innocent. In fact, she told him that she had let Tunji know she had a boyfriend. All this did not please Olumide. His fiery temper was set ablaze.

'Teju, I just want you to accept that you have done me wrong.'

'How could you say that, Olu? Tunji recognised me because of that party. We are more or less like acquaintances, that is all. I am sorry if you are hurt, but I still don't think my behaviour was in any way bad.'

147

'There you go again, Teju. How would you have felt to be told by a girlfriend of yours that I dated some other girl? Also, I have the feeling that had I not mentioned this issue, you would have been silent about it.'

'Exactly. Because as I said, it is nothing to me since he is nothing special to me. Also, I would not have reacted this way if I were in your shoes. Firstly, I ought to trust you, and secondly, you are entitled to some casual acquaintances, whether male or female.'

'So you are not apologetic and sober about the whole situation? Is this what you have to tell me by way of an explanation?' Olumide asked hotly.

'Olu, if you trust me and know what you mean to me, you ought not to talk to me like this. It is not fair at all.'

'*En-en,* you mean you are indirectly wanting me to give you license for infidelity? You are mad!' Olu shouted.

With that said, Olumide walked off on Teju. In his heart, he knew that Teju would come and beg him. She would make him some nice pancakes and meat. Till then, he was going to stay put. Luckily, Teju had been alone in her room when Olumide visited. Her other roommates were all out to their various pursuits. Probably, if they had been in, Olumide and Teju would not have been chanced to get very angry with each other. Throughout that week, Olumide and Teju did not see each other. Neither of them felt they were in the wrong, and each had expected the other to apologise first.

During that week of malice between Olumide and Teju, Tunji called on Teju four times. On one of those occasions, Tunji had persuaded Teju to know his room at Fajuyi, and he was successful. On that very occasion of Teju to Tunji's room, Lana was in but without Shade.

'Paddy,' Tunji hailed Lana, 'please meet Teju Akinola.'

'Teju, you are welcome, and let me assure you that you are in the good hands of a gentleman.'

Everybody laughed to Lana's remark.

'Yes, that reminds me,' Tunji began, 'Lana have you seen your letter?'

'No, which letter?' Lana asked seriously.

'Oh, then it is still on the Porter's Lodge. Just look on the desk. I had meant to pick it up, but somehow it escaped my mind.'

'Tunji, no problem, I'll go for it. You know, I don't blame you. How could you have remembered with an angel like Teju besides you?'

Both Tunji and Lana had laughed, but Teju was embarrassed. She became more so after Lana had left the room. Tunji put her at ease by talking briefly on certain topics especially from his medical experiences.

After a few minutes, he said, 'So this is where I stay, Teju. Now that you have known my room, I need not delay you any further.'

'All right. I will call in once in a while. Do you know Olumide Fadipe, my friend? He is on the topmost floor in room 312. Two of you must meet sometime. You'll both make nice friends, I think.'

No answer from Tunji. He led the way out of the room and stood with his back against the door as if to barricade her from going out. His eyes expressed all the deep feelings he had for Teju. His hands were folded in front of his chest. His lips were pointed in a queer way.

'Tunji, what do you mean by all this?' Teju asked feeling a bit uneasy.

No answer.

'Tunji, I want to go. Please let me pass. You are scaring me. I won't come here again.'

'Please, Teju,' Tunji said softly. 'Only a kiss,' he whispered.

'Not today,' Teju answered back.

There was a bit of forceful play as Tunji tried to embrace her. Teju was one of those girls who did not succumb easily when the relationship was still very fresh. After two minutes of speechless wrestling, Tunji stopped.

'Teju, I love you so much. I am very sincere. I have no one in my life. If you don't throw me away, you will discover it is true.'

'Tunji, we are friends, aren't we? We are not enemies.'

'I know, Teju. I only want you to know how I feel for you. It is something much more than ordinary friendship.'

'Okay, I understand you. I will appreciate these feelings. Just have patience with me.'

Teju had felt excited that night in her room. She did not really know why. She had a vague idea deep in her mind about what she was letting herself into, but she could not control it. She felt very different about Tunji. It was not like the way she felt about Olumide for a period of about ten months. They were course mates. They had begun as academic friends. The relationship between them started when Olumide began visiting Teju in her room and Teju also returning the visits. And that was all to it.

The following week, Olumide decided to break the ice first, maybe for the reason of needing a woman's company and warmth after such a long absence. When he got to Teju's room, he noticed three things about her. He saw that she did not look excited about his having to come to her first. Secondly, she did not look sober, and thirdly, she was in no mood to impress him. Olumide ignored these negative airs Teju set to rebuff him.

He embraced her and then in the vernacular he said, 'Teju, my wife, who is hotter than fire. So how are we? You were really in for a long battle. You don't want to say anything?'

'Olumide, what do you want to hear from me again that you have not heard and have not wanted to hear?' She asked unsmilingly.

There was a knock on the door. Titi, one of Teju's roommates who was in, ushered in the knocker. It happened to be a gentleman who was all smiles and had a bunch of beautiful artificial flowers in his hand. It was Tunji. He greeted everyone in the room in a general way with a wave of his left hand and a big smile on his face to hide his uneasiness which was caused by Olumide's presence. Teju was excited.

'Is that for my corner, Tunji?'

'Of course! For whom else in this world would I bring flowers to?' Tunji asked as he sat himself on Teju's vacant chair.

Olumide who was seated on the bed was so shocked that he was just looking at Tunji as if he was not a human being.

At last, he was able to control himself.

'Oh, you both know each other this well?'

'Ah, yes,' said Tunji. 'Are you Olumide? I am Tunji.'

'I know you are Tunji, but what right have you to visit my girlfriend just like that?'

'Exchange is no robbery.'

Chapter 15
The Maiden Trip

You have done great things… **Psalm 71:19**

How does one start this story? What is really fantastic about going to London? Many of us were born there and many of us have been there several times. However, it will make an interesting read about how a child visited London when he is a grown-up adult of thirty-five years.

First of all, there was the week before the journey. It was pregnant with premonitions: fear of foreign exchange, visa, passport, travellers' cheque and fear of the unknown. This week hatched out successfully with no disruptions other than to falsify the premonitions.

Then the actual day of travelling came. It was on a Sunday. I was with my husband in bed. We were going to leave for Lagos at 7:30 am. The flight to London actually was scheduled for 12 noon that day. It was still black dawn, say about 3:30 am.

'My dear, are you awake?' I asked my husband.

I am a light sleeper. In fact, to say, I am a light sleeper is to be modest. I often suffer from insomnia which I inherited from my father. The peaceful solemnity of my husband's frame told me he was not asleep: no heavy heaves, no snoring and no fast breathing...

'Yes,' he replied. 'Shouldn't we start to prepare now? I haven't ironed the shirt I want to wear.'

'Oh, my dear, it is still too early! We can start to prepare at about five.'

The advice didn't work. It was just like my husband—too proud to admit that his wife's opinion was more reasonable than his. At last by 7:30 am, we were ready to leave for Lagos. We had a suitcase in between us. In the suitcase, my husband stuffed in five ties, one housecoat, one bed sheet, one covering cloth, three trousers, three shirts, two towels, two blankets, a couple of undies and my two dresses.

'Oh grief!' Shade, my junior sister despaired at the weight of the suitcase. 'Brother Sayo and Sister Christy, what have you got in here? This box is already more than 60 kg!'

In the end, most of the items were chucked out of the box to leave two garments for each of us for our usage. She was also shocked that I was attired in native clothing and urged me with great persuasion to dress English.

At Lagos, the moment of relief came when the suitcase was checked in along with the bag that contained *garri*, melon, crayfish, pepper and *ogbono*—all foodstuffs for our host in London. Also, there was no problem as to whether we had incomplete documents or foreign exchange on us. Having gone through this, we waved at my dad and sister who had accompanied us to Lagos.

For my husband, the moment of reality came when we were seated in the Nigerian Airways plane by 2 pm. The plane had not left by 12 because it had no fuel. Soon the plane began to warm up. My husband's eyes were fixed out of the window at where he sat. He looked very concerned and worried. He directed my attention to the plane's wing.

'Darling, we are not safe. This plane is not a good one. Its wing is spoilt. Do you think they are aware of this? Should I notify them quickly?'

'Oh no, my dear. Don't worry. The wings are made like that. The flaps open and close once in a while. It is nothing. Even the foreign aircrafts have it this way,' I said soothingly.

After this, I laughed off my guts, more so because my husband tightened his belt. I told him it was not necessary at all to fasten the seatbelt before the plane took off.

By 3 pm, the plane took off. My husband exchanged glances with me. The seatbelt was held securely tight over his belly. I could understand how he felt. His eyes had read, 'So at last!' The previous weeks had all flown so fast making the events seem like a dream come into reality. There had been moments of doubt, anger, indecisions, mistakes, anxiety and over-eagerness pertaining to the preparations and arrangements for the trip.

After some time, while we were still in the air, people were moving up and down. My husband had been impressed with the earphones supplied for the enjoyment of music. I watched him as he touched and toyed with all the various buttons on the armrest of his seat. All the time I spoke to him, the earphones never left his head. Sometimes, he did not hear me well and would nod his head for no reason. I would then remove the earphone from his head and say whatever I really wanted him to hear from me.

Then my husband felt it was time to visit the plane's loo. I watched him unfasten his seatbelt and make unsteady steps to the loo. I saw him wait endlessly in front of the first loo.

When he realised that there was more than one, he began to bang at the door of the loo he had been waiting at. After I had calmed myself from my fits of laughter, I walked over to him and pointed out a sign on the door latch that read 'Occupied' and walked back to my seat.

Mealtime came. I fancied the portable plates and cutlery we were served with. I told my husband to give me his share so that I could use my serviette to clean them up and thrust into my handbag. He welcomed the idea. Night time was a bit bad for me. I was hardly comfortable enough to sleep. Try as I could, I couldn't sleep much. My husband had no problem. Several times, he dozed off, but then he would quickly wake up in a fit. He did not want to sleep in the air. To him, it was "risky". 'Anything could happen,' he had said.

Eventually, we got to London. My husband craned his neck to take in the beautiful sight of the city which as at 8 pm was not yet enshrouded with darkness. After the final hassle of immigration, customs and checking were over, the next problem beset us. How were we to reach at our host's end? My husband while in Nigeria is "master of the roads" and "king of all directions". He hardly ever missed his way; no matter if he was a stranger. He probably thought the same gift of articulatory devices could be employed in London. The map in my hand was ignored. The advice given to us by certain people in Nigeria was flung carelessly to the winds. I knew I was in for a rough time. I love to rely on asking questions from people around, but my husband isn't like that.

Outside Heathrow Airport premises, my husband advised that we entered an airport bus going to Terminal 4. The driver received £10 from my husband and gave him his change. At the backseat, my husband did not know how much he was given. I also felt that he had been cheated especially as we both reasoned along the terms of pounds, shillings and pence. Finally, we gave the money to someone on the bus to count for us. This person said the change was £9.40p. It was not £9.15 shillings as we had expected. At Terminal 4, we were advised to go back to Terminal 1. There, we were advised to take the tube transport to Victoria. In the end, through a lot of enquiries from people I asked, we got to our destination very late by 3 am.

When I think of the amount of energy we lost walking on empty roads, meeting people who could not understand our questions because they themselves were strangers or non-Briton, hailing buses filled with amused people, I cannot but remember how close to tears I was with frustration and how close to doom my husband felt.

Later on, at our hosts' after a very nice meal, we settled for the night. Now we could joke about our moments out in the cold night of London battling with trying to locate our host. Our host lived almost two hours from the airport in the outskirts of London.

'It is good to be home and feel safe. Move nearer to me my dear,' my husband said in high spirits.

I felt amused, especially when I had cause to remember how irritated he felt at my asking questions from every Dick and Harry. At times, in the tubes, he would prefer to stand out of sheer anger. All the same, I moved nearer. Our room was cosy, neatly furnished, rugged all round, had a big spring soft bed with a TV set.

'Darling, you were so tensed a few hours ago. I am glad it is all over now,' I said.

'You know what? I saw some bad-faced looking guys. They reminded me of those guys we watch on TV who kill for no purpose.'

'Just your imagination, darling,' I said.

'You can say that again. What made me mad with you was taking strangers to confidence about directions. Some of them really looked like crooks. I felt we were near our doom. Imagine coming across some of those crooks on those deserted streets we walked through.'

'No, darling, my instincts would have warned me. I believe in asking people questions when I am in difficulty.'

My husband hugged me closer, and that ended it all.